Away From Yesterday

Away From Yesterday

SOMETIMES MOVING FORWARD MEANS GOING BACK…

Chanelle Fairlene Pillay

ISBN: 9798650243687

Front Photographic Image: Brett Patzke

Scripture quotations taken from the King James Version of the Bible.

This book is a work of fiction. Names, characters, places and incidents are either a product of the author's imagination or are used fictitiously. Any resemblance to actual people living or dead, events or locales is entirely coincidental.

Thank You

To my Savior, Jesus Christ; without whom I am nothing, and can do nothing without. May every dream and gift that You have given me always point to You…

To The SuperNatural Church of Jesus Christ; a ministry that has dynamically shifted and unlocked my mindset, my purpose, and my experiences with the Lord…

To my Dad, Mom, Sister and Brother; for all your unwavering love, support, encouragement and continuous prayers and input through my life. You have always stood by and cheered me on to be and do all that God has purposed…

To my Grandparents, Mamma and Papa; for teaching me about Jesus as a little girl, and for all the prayers you sowed into my life which are being reaped now. I look forward to meeting you at the gates of eternity one day…

"The LORD says it is not over: The book is not closed in your life. He says, Behold, there are many books of your life and many books, the LORD says, that you yourself will write as well. And people will know of My character and people will know about Me, for up until this time they have heard about Me, but they will know Me from the books that which will come from you…"

Prophetic word released from THE LORD through Prophet Adrian EliJAH Robert,
10 February 2019
The SuperNatural Church of Jesus Christ
Johannesburg
South Africa

"There is therefore now no condemnation to them which are in Christ Jesus…"

Romans 8:1

One

The headlights of the truck blinded him just as the force of the impact met the vehicle. The sound of crushing metal ripped through his sleep, jolting him upright in bed. Tyler felt his body drenched in sweat, and his breathing labored. The nightmare was vivid. As if he were reliving the accident from twelve years ago all over again. Despite the many years that had rolled by, the flashbacks still stalked him.

The figure next to him shuffled underneath the sheets. Tyler caught a glimpse of her freckled face. Her strawberry blonde hair was strewn across his pillow. He couldn't recall her name, although he remembered mingling with her for a few minutes at the business party before bringing her back to his apartment for the night. A familiar pang of guilt pricked his gut, but he dismissed it. It was not the first time he had done something like this over the years. Whenever he grew tired of spending his nights alone with his destitute heart and the waves of guilt, a beautiful woman or a couple of drinks usually kept him company.

He reached for his cellphone on the bedside table and un-locked it to check the time. *01:18.* An eerie chill worked its way down his spine and his insides twisted as he stared at the digits on his screen again. Over the years, Tyler had convinced himself that it was either a coincidence or that his body was programmed to wake up at that precise time. It happened regularly since the night of the accident, and Tyler was unable to make sense of it. He threw the bedsheet off of him and carefully made his way around the discarded clothes on the floor towards his bedroom window.

He peered outside the window of his 20th floor apartment building. His head still throbbed from the blaring of music and drinks from several hours before. The street lamps lit the road below, and Tyler watched as a few cars drove by. He drew a deep breath. The flashbacks and memories were more frequent now than they had ever been before. It was unavoidable every time Tyler closed his eyes to rest. He couldn't remember the last time when he had slept peacefully through the night.

"To have peace, one must know the Prince of Peace…"

Tyler spun around at the voice, his senses heightened, and on edge. But there was nobody there. He was just met with darkness and the occasional revving of a car outside his building. He felt his heart slam against his chest. He was almost convinced that some-one had just spoken to him as clear as day.

To have peace, one must know the Prince of Peace? Tyler repeated the words in his head. He let out a frustrated huff, wondering where the Prince of Peace had been twelve years ago when He was needed the most. What Tyler lacked in peace, he made up for with sleeping pills, alcohol, business parties, and women- all were better outlets than facing the raging tempest within him. Even if peace was what he desired, Tyler felt unworthy to receive it.

Not after all I've done, he thought.

He walked towards the kitchen, grabbing an empty high-ball-glass from the counter. He held it underneath the tap as the water slowly started filling it. The glass triggered an involuntary memory in him- a famous sermon preached by his father during a Sunday morning church service many years ago.

"Is the glass of your life half-full or half-empty?"

His father had asked that question in his message. It was a message intended to encourage people to find the gratitude in all seasons, rather than focus on their pain. Tyler had believed the words back then, when life was perfect. But when the unthinkable occurred, it was impossible for him to make sense of anything good amidst the overwhelming sorrow.

He looked at the glass in his hand. He wondered if he were to shatter it to pieces if anyone would be crazy enough to still want to use it. That was precisely how his life felt; each broken piece reflected the pain, condemnation, and disappointment from twelve years ago. His glass of life was not half-full or half-empty. He was just empty; a shell of a man.

Back then, at nineteen, Tyler had many aspirations for the future. He was brought up in a Christian home where his family had instilled spiritual principles and faith-based values as best they could in him. He was a top achiever in his first year of college. And he was in love with the most amazing girl- his best friend. The memory of her brought with it a deep ache in him.

I wonder if you've forgotten me, Emmy, he thought.

The sound of the running water snapped him away from her face, and he turned the tap off, letting out a sigh in the process. He assumed that the anxiety rising within him was because of his grandfather's death, and the inescapable reality that he had to return to his hometown for the funeral. The thought alone made him feel physically sick. He gulped the water back, trying to cool himself down.

He thought about his grandfather. Tyler closed his eyes, picturing himself at his grandad's house again, all those years ago. It had been Tyler's dream home. He recalled it as a quaint double-story building situated on a large property and nestled among countless towering trees. Tyler could almost hear the trickling of the little stream that ran through the backyard, and the feel of the wet stones and pebbles in his hand. His grand plan had been to finish college, get a job, move in with his grandfather, buy the house from him, and then marry Emily. Tyler recalled how his grandfather would tilt his head back, laughing at Tyler's plan, before wiggling his finger at him and saying in his deep voice, *"Now that's a deal, my boy! I'll keep this place in tip-top shape just for you."*

Tyler leaned forward at the counter, his head hanging low. He thought back to the last phone call conversation with his grandfather. It had been several weeks ago, just before his health had rapidly declined. His grandfather had chuckled, saying that he would be sure to make the trip to see Tyler soon. Tyler felt the remorse well up within him. That trip never came. Tyler had missed the chance at saying goodbye.

Leaving everything behind had been a difficult, but necessary decision for Tyler. Although he was only several hours away from his hometown, he felt a lifetime apart from it all. He believed that there was no place on earth that he could disappear to after what he had done to everyone he loved.

His parents had probably assumed that he would return after graduating from college- after the dust of the hurt had settled. After all, people claimed that time healed all wounds. But they were wrong. No amount of time could heal his wounds. And no amount of time could provide him with a clean slate after the events of that night had changed all their lives forever.

"Though your sins be as scarlet, they shall be as white as snow..."

Again, Tyler almost lost his balance at the sound of the voice. He felt his brows knit together as he scanned the room again. Besides the woman in his bed, there was nobody else there with him.

Just breathe, you're stressed out and hearing things, he told himself.

He made his way across the glossy wooden floors to the bedside table. He reached for the sleeping pills and popped the lid open, dusting two little white beads into the palm of his hand. He stared at them for a while, wondering if they would come through for him this time and relieve him of his burdens for a few more hours. He threw two into his mouth and positioned his head back, swallowing them. He maneuvered carefully under the bedsheet and turned his back to the sleeping woman. He hoped that he would wake up before sunrise to get his morning workout in. In that way, he could also avoid forced conversations with the stranger.

Emily's face resurfaced in his mind again, returning the heaviness in his chest. Tyler remembered the way her sweet voice had resonated through the darkness when he was regaining consciousness in the hospital. She had whispered close to his ear, saying, *"Tyler, I'm right here with you. I'm not going to leave you."*

Tyler squeezed his eyes shut, trying to forget the distant memory. He was grateful that the sleeping pills were starting to take effect. His guilty conscience made it hard for him to breathe whenever he thought about the pain he had caused her.

There were days when he allowed himself to wander back to the pages of yesterday. All sorts of questions would be scribbled across his mind. Had he made the right choice in leaving? Should he have stayed and sought help from his family? Had it been necessary to break the heart of the only girl he had ever loved?

Although these questions plagued him endlessly, there was one thing Tyler knew he had been right in doing. And that was walking away from the faith he once believed in. It had been heartbreaking to leave the family and girl he loved. But it had been easy turning his back on the God they all believed in.

Simply, because, none of his father's sermons, and none of the Bible promises had been enough to change that night. None of what Tyler was taught to believe about God and His plans had proven true when it mattered the most.

Although Tyler was angry at God for allowing tragedy to strike that night in claiming the life of his brother, there was one person who Tyler knew was the real cause of Noah's death.

And that was him.

Two

eth folded the last program containing the order of the funeral service and laid it on the church entrance table. The photograph she had chosen of her father-in-law was one of her favorites. She could still see the wisdom in his eyes and found herself returning his contagious smile. At ninety years old, Bill had lived a full and fulfilled life. There was only one thing that he had waited patiently for, which he did not get the opportunity to witness.

And that was Tyler coming back home.

The sorrow overwhelmed her heart as she looked over at Bill's empty seat in the aisle of the second row. She would miss him terribly. Yet, with certainty, she also knew that he now had the most magnificent seat of all- in eternity with the Lord.

Michael was sitting nearby, penning down the contents of his message for the funeral. He was the strongest man Beth had ever known. Despite the losses in his life, Michael always found the blessings in every situation. His father's passing had been rough on him. They had been close, ever since Michael had lost his mother as a little boy. Beth knew that despite one's age, it was never easy burying a parent. She felt her breath catch in her throat.

Or a child, she thought.

Michael's gaze found hers, and the corners of his mouth lifted ever so slightly. His eyes held a shimmer of grief and longing. Beth did not have to ask what he was thinking. After forty years of marriage, they knew each other as well as their reflections. The last time they had to bury a family member was twelve years ago. And that loss had come without warning, like a thief in the night. In one moment, everything came crumbling down. The corners of her eyes stung with tears. No matter how many years had passed, the thought of that loss still yanked her back to the floor of that hospital waiting room.

Many people had comforted them in the months that followed losing their eldest son, Noah. What many of those people did not realize was that their family hadn't just lost Noah that night. They had lost Tyler too. Life had dealt them all a horrific and unexpected blow. And navigating the days after that had been a hellacious challenge.

Their faith was tested like never before. Beth and Michael found themselves clinging to God with every last bit of strength they had. They didn't do it because it was expected of them as ministers. Losing Noah had ripped their lives right down the center like a torn photograph. Yet, despite their heartache, they had a peace knowing that Noah was with the Lord and that they would surely see him again. That was the only comfort that helped Beth get out of bed every morning and forge ahead.

Beth remembered how Michael had comforted her with a story from the Bible on King David. When King David and his wife, Bathsheba, had lost their first child together, his mourning ceased the moment the tragic news was received. King David knew that although his child would not return to them, they would see their child's face at the gates of eternity when they were one day called Home.

Believing in Jesus gave one the confidence that death was the beginning of a better life; a life of no pain, sorrow, or tragedy. A life that both Noah and Bill were now living. The reminder of that truth brought an unspeakable joy to Beth's heart.

The face of Tyler, her youngest son, flashed before her eyes. He, on the other hand, had turned his back on everything and everyone. He rebelled, letting all that he once believed in fall by the wayside in his pursuit of worldly pleasures to fill the void in his life. He had not returned home once- not for a single weekend visit or even a thanksgiving holiday. Beth and Michael had to often travel to visit him over the years- whenever their church schedules permitted them. And every time they left him, they grew more burdened at how far adrift he was in his ocean of pain.

Although Beth was pleased with her son's accomplishments -being the youngest director in a large marketing corporation- she cared more about his spiritual and personal life, both of which were in ruins at thirty-one years old. The night of the accident had changed his perspective on everything, causing him to find solace in all the wrong places and with questionable company. There was not a day that passed where Beth and Michael did not feel the heaviness in their hearts about the state of their youngest son's soul.

Beth scanned the empty seats in the church and felt a lump form in her throat. *Lord, here we are preaching to and encouraging others, yet our own son is lost*, she thought.

Bill's photograph caught her attention again. It was positioned at the front of the church where the casket was to stand the next day. Beth remembered their last conversation together about Tyler. Whilst sipping his lemonade on the front porch, Bill had spoken with such confidence, saying, *"In the fight between condemnation and grace, God's grace will always triumph. Don't lose hope, Beth. A true son will always find his way home."*

Beth hoped he was right. Hope was all she had to hold onto.

"Beth, is there anything else I can do to help?" The voice of Emily interrupted Beth's thoughts. She was glad for that. She needed something else to take her mind off of all life's burdens. She turned and smiled at the young woman standing in front of her; a woman Beth had once believed would be her daughter-in-law.

"Thank you so much for your help, Em." Beth clasped Emily's hands in her own, mindful of the significant diamond engagement ring on Emily's finger. Beth motioned towards Michael and kept her voice soft. "We should be leaving shortly once Pastor Mike finishes preparing for the service. You and Ian can lock up the church then."

Emily smiled sweetly, responding, "There's no rush. Ian is at a business meeting in any event." She checked her wristwatch, adding, "He should be on his way soon."

Ian was Emily's fiancé. When Ian had joined the church a few years back, his sights had been immediately set on Emily. Everyone knew that Emily and Ian would make a good match. Emily had a passion for the youth ministry in their church, which Ian fully supported her in. He was pleasant, and charming. Always ready to step in and help when called upon. They were planning to marry in a few months. Still, despite Ian's admirable qualities and how evident his love for Emily was, Beth and Michael knew who truly held Emily's heart all through the years.

From the time that Beth could remember, Emily was running through their house, her laughter resounding from their garden. She had been joined at the hip with both Tyler and Noah from the time they were children- especially Tyler. It wasn't a surprise when their childhood bond blossomed into something innocent and special in their teenage years. Both sets of parents had approved of their relationship, excited about what the future would bring to them.

Emily was the daughter that Beth and Michael never had. And Tyler was smitten with her. Nothing had been able to tear them away from each other.

Nothing until that night, Beth thought.

Michael approached them both, flipping his notepad closed and popping his pen in his shirt pocket.

Emily put her arms around him and embraced him warmly. "I'm sorry for your loss, Pastor Mike. Uncle Bill was the best." Her voice was thick with emotion, and Beth saw the despair fall across Michael's face as well.

He squeezed Emily's shoulders as he stood next to her. His voice was choked up when he responded. "Our loss, but heavens gain." He exchanged a knowing look with Beth and then focused back on Emily. "Thank you for all your help with the arrangements and church set up. We can always count on you to put things together at the last minute. Some of the youth graciously gave up their time too." He paused and squeezed her again. "The Lord is using you to do great things with them, Em."

Emily sniffed back her tears. "God is doing it all." She leaned in close to him and said, "And that's what family is for."

Beth smiled at her. Emily was right- this was what family was. If only Tyler knew how incomplete they were without him.

Michael checked his watch, asking, "Speaking of family, what time is Tyler's flight arriving?"

Beth knew that Michael meant no harm in asking about Tyler in Emily's presence. Being occupied with the funeral service, and dealing with the loss of his father made him forget the sensitivity of the situation. Beth kept her tone casual and she tried to not look at Emily's face when she answered her husband.

"He should be arriving tomorrow morning. He said it's not necessary to pick him up. He will see us at the service."

Michael nodded slowly. "Did he say how long he plans on staying?"

Beth shrugged. "He said he took a few days off, so your guess is as good as mine. You know how he can be."

Michael let out a tired-sounding sigh at her answer. His phone started to ring, breaking the silence between them. He lifted his finger, excusing himself as he took the call to the side. Beth allowed her eyes to fall on Emily, whose face had paled several shades lighter.

Emily's voice was a weak whisper when she spoke next. "Beth, I'll be right back. I just need some air."

Beth watched her walk away, and her heart went out to her. *Poor girl*, she thought. She knew Emily's world had just been shifted off its axis. She inhaled and allowed her eyes to wander to the front of the church, where a wooden cross framed the wall behind the altar.

The scripture engraved on the wall was from 1 Corinthians 13:13. It was one of Beth's favorites. It said, *And now these three remain: faith, hope and love. But the greatest of these is love…*

Beth pressed her lips together. The words were true, yet weighed heavily in her spirit. She knew that the coming days would truly try them all. They were going to need all the faith, hope, and love possible.

Faith- for God to get them through.

Hope- for things to change.

And love. For Tyler to remember the greatest love of all.

Three

mily felt suffocated.

The pathway before her looked as if it were spinning. Her palms felt clammy, and she could hear her own heart pounding in her chest. She hoped that her flabbergasted reaction to the news had gone unnoticed.

His name alone had rattled her unexpectedly.

She needed to sit down, and the closest spot to do that was the white bench outside the church, which overlooked the fish pond. It was the last place she should have sat, especially if she wanted to rid him from her thoughts at that moment. The bench alone whispered the memories of their teenage years as she approached it. Emily found her spot on the one end and took a deep breath. She let her gaze fall to the space on the bench beside her. It mirrored the secret emptiness that had formed in her heart since she was nineteen.

Tyler was returning after twelve years. She let that reality sink in for a moment. Her emotions were conflicted. She couldn't recognize if it was anxiety, anger or delight that wrestled within her. It felt like a lifetime had passed since their voices had mingled with each other.

From the moment they had said goodbye at the airport, Emily had felt as if a piece of her heart had departed on that flight with him, and it had never returned. All he had given her in exchange for their years together was a simple break-up text. She remembered the text message word for word. It had embedded itself in her heart, the familiar sting often returning every time she replayed it.

Emmy. I've been thinking a lot this week. This is not fair for both of us. Things will never be as they once were. It's best we go our separate ways. Please don't call or text. Move on with your life. I have with mine. I'm sorry for doing this now and like this. It's just better this way. Goodbye.

Emily clenched her fists at the memory of the message. How had he dared to make such a decision on a whim and cut her off like she was nothing? She remembered defying his request by trying to call, text, email, and reach out on social media. All had been hours of her wasted time and energy. He had changed his details, deactivated his accounts, and had made his parents promise to not give her his new information. Emily chose not to put Beth and Michael in the middle of the situation and cause them any more stress than they were already experiencing with all that had happened in their family.

Weeks, months, and years had passed where Emily would

jump at the sound of a notification or ring of her cellphone- desperately hoping it was from him. She wished he would appear out of thin air and tell her that he was wrong for leaving her, and that he still loved her. But instead, his silence spoke more than words ever could.

Michael and Beth exited the church doors, and Emily tried to compose herself. She didn't want them to worry. They were dealing with enough concerns and grief. She watched them walk towards their car, holding hands. Emily was in awe of how close they still were despite the tragedy and brokenness that had paved their lives.

Emily sighed. *Tyler, that could have been us*, she thought.

Beth looked over her shoulder when she reached the car and did a small goodbye-wave at Emily. Emily smiled weakly, and Beth returned it with a reassuring nod. As if she knew what Emily's heart was going through.

Beth had been a witness to how broken Emily was when Tyler had left. Emily had even questioned whether Tyler had blamed her for what had happened that tragic night.

Beth's words still rang in her ears. *"The only person that he blames is himself"*, she had said.

Emily hadn't been satisfied with that answer. She knew that if she ever had the chance to come face to face with Tyler again, she would ask him herself. Blaming her was the only plausible explanation for why he had treated her like she meant nothing to him.

Emily felt hot tears blur her vision. She had loved Tyler from the moment she knew what love was. At the age of fourteen, her heart had made up its mind. He was the one for her. They had so many dreams and hopes for the future, until one night ripped it all out away from them.

Losing Noah had been a devastating blow to their family, their church, and in the community. She recalled Pastor Mike's famous sermon about looking at the glass as half-full in every situation. For years, Emily had tried to find the good in what had happened between them. Until one day, she found just a sliver of it.

Even though Tyler was not in her life, Emily had to remind herself that he was still alive and healthy. The accident could have been worse. It could have claimed Tyler's life too. And as long as Tyler was still breathing, there was still a chance that he would return to all of them.

Holding onto that hope was one thing. The waiting part was the hard reality. No matter how many seasons had drifted on by, Emily had not been capable of untangling Tyler from her heart. It was probably what losing a limb felt like; life had to go on, but it would always be missing something significant.

A gust of wind disheveled her hair, and Emily pulled the strands to the side and hugged herself, whispering a prayer, "*Lord, please give me the strength to face what's to come.*"

Immediately, a warmth came over her, accompanied by a reminder from the Word of God. It resonated within her spirit.

Be still and know that I am God.

Emily closed her eyes and focused on that scripture. God was still on the throne, and He still held her tomorrows. Even though the one person she had loved with all her heart had walked away from her, Emily knew that God would never leave her.

The hoot of a car made Emily jump. She looked over and saw Ian getting off his vehicle. He was dressed in his suit, having been in meetings the entire day. The sight of him brought a surge of guilt in her. Here she was, engaged to the perfect man, yet sitting on an old church bench, thinking back to her first love and the days that had passed. Days that were still hidden in her heart.

She left the spot on the bench and met Ian halfway down the path. He grinned when he saw her, kissing her cheek lightly, saying, "Sorry I'm late, baby. We had to revise the presentation for next week." He took out a set of church keys that jingled in his hands as he made his way to the front doors.

Emily smiled, following closely behind him and trying her best to be normal. "It's okay. Pastor Mike and Beth just pulled out a few minutes ago."

"How's Pastor Mike holding up? It must be tough for him to plan his own father's funeral." He locked the doors and continued, "I couldn't imagine doing that." He turned the alarm system on before wrapping his arm around her shoulders. Emily leaned in closer to his side and walked alongside him towards the car. He opened the passenger door for her to get in before lightly jogging around the front of the BMW and sliding into the driver's seat next to her.

"Do you want to grab some lunch before I head back to the office? You must be starving." He turned the radio down before continuing. "You've been here the entire morning preparing for tomorrow's service."

Emily swallowed the lump in her throat. *No amount of preparation will be enough for tomorrow*, she thought.

They exited the church driveway, and Emily nervously twisted the engagement ring on her finger as she stared out the window. It was not a good idea to go for lunch with Ian while being consumed with anxieties about the following day. She didn't want to talk to Ian about it either.

What would she possibly say? That the young man who had left her broken and pining for him for years was coming back to town for his grandfather's funeral? And that she couldn't breathe at the mere thought of his return?

Ian knew as much as he needed to know about Tyler. He didn't need to know the secrets in her heart- there were far too many of those.

Emily tried to keep her tone light. "Actually, could you drop me off at the coffee shop? I need to do some banking and lock up. Candice is leaving early today."

Ian didn't seem to pick up on anything unusual from her request. He transitioned onto the fast lane. "Sure, then maybe we could grab dinner later tonight? Once tomorrow comes, things will be difficult."

Emily swiped him a perplexed look. *What does he mean by that?* she wondered. Ian's eyes were ahead on the road, but he reached for her hand.

"My flight leaves out after the funeral, remember?" He frowned slightly.

Emily felt horrible again. Her paranoia had made her forget

that he was going away for a few days for a business event, and that's what he had meant in his comment.

She let out a frustrated groan. "Yes, I remember," she said, with an apologetic smile. "I'm sorry. I just went blank for a bit. There's a lot on my mind."

He smiled and kissed the palm of her hand, his tone teasing as he replied, "As long as it's not about leaving me standing alone at the altar in a few months."

The heat crept into Emily's cheeks. On a typical day, she would have thrown her head back laughing, but today, his words stirred an uneasiness in her. She forced a smile and squeezed his hand. "No, it's not that."

Ian returned her smile and kept his eyes on the road. His voice was still humorous. "Good, because everyone knows how long it took for you to say yes in the first place."

Emily didn't need reminding. Many people had believed she was crazy for not dating Ian when he had relentlessly pursued her in the beginning. Emily didn't blame them. How were people to know that she had only ever dreamt of Tyler standing at the front of a wedding aisle waiting for her? But not all dreams came true.

Tyler was her past. Ian was her future. She had chosen Ian because she felt safe with him. And because loving him was easy. Ian didn't have any horrible surprises waiting around the corner to creep up on her. Emily knew that it was unlikely she would ever wake up to a text message from her fiancé that said goodbye- with no further explanation or care in the world. Ian loved the Lord, and he loved her. What more could she ask for?

Ian pulled the car into an available parking spot right outside her café. Emily looked up at the name of her business.

Emmy's

Her heart fluttered. To this day, Emily had never shared the reason why her coffee shop was named *Emmy's*. Only one person had ever called her by that name. And she could almost hear the sound of his voice saying it.

A few regular customers exited the store with their takeaway boxes in hand. They caught her gaze as they walked past the car and waved cheerfully. Emily smiled and waved back. In a close-knit neighborhood, everybody felt like family. Through the tall glass windows of the café, Emily could see it was a busy day. She turned to Ian, who was scrolling through his phone's calendar and mouthing something to himself. The sunlight glistened off his dark blonde hair, and Emily understood why he turned the heads of so many women.

"I'll see you later, then?" She leaned across the center compartment and kissed his cheek lightly. He instantly put his phone away, and just before she could open the car door to step out, he drew her closer to him by the nape of her neck. His lips touched hers as he brushed a strand of her hair behind her ears. That gesture didn't feel the same as when Tyler used to do it.

Emily chastised herself. What was wrong with her? Her thoughts had been running rampant since the news of his return.

Ian smiled at her, pulling back, oblivious to her internal struggles. "I love you, Em."

Emily felt that suffocating sensation overpower her again. She returned his kiss with another quick one before smiling back, saying, "I know."

She opened the car door and waved to him as she made her way through the doors of her café. She watched his car drive off and felt a sigh of relief come over her. A part of her felt awful for not returning those three particular words to him when he had said it. But today was different.

How was she to say those words to her fiancé when the face of Tyler Hill burned in her mind?

Emily entered the coffee shop and greeted a few of her regular customers. She noticed some students were busy studying over their waffles in a corner booth. There was also the familiar elderly couple sharing a slice of cheesecake while watching people pass by on the outside street. Emily could smell the cinnamon wafting in from the kitchen. Two servers exited the doors carrying plates of croissants and sandwiches for a nearby table.

Candice- one of Emily's good friends and her appointed manager- was wiping down a table when she saw Emily come in.

Candice grinned, a surprised look making its way across her face. "Emily! What's up? It's your day off!" She paused, and her blue eyes suddenly grew wider. "Wait, did one of the customers call you to complain?" She didn't wait for Emily to answer before rattling off, asking, "Was it Mr. Brooks?"

Emily let out a genuine laugh for the first time that afternoon, and made her way around the counter to the system. "No, Mr. Brooks did not complain." Her eyes darted to Candice, suspiciously. "But, why would you think that? What did you do to Mr. Brooks?"

Candice shrugged and leaned against the counter, the usual cheerful beat in her voice. "Let's not talk about that, let's talk about you!" She gave Emily a playful poke on the shoulder before saying, "You got that handsome fiancé leaving on business, and you would rather be here than with him?" She tilted her head. "Did you guys have some sort of fight? Is that what happened?"

Emily shook her head and had a quick look at the sales for that day while keeping her voice low. "No, we didn't have a fight."

Candice didn't seem convinced. Ever since Candice had started working at *Emmy's,* Emily had grown quite fond of her. Candice always said exactly what was on her mind. She was an acquired taste, as she sometimes put it.

Emily blew at a wisp of her hair. "Tyler is coming back tomorrow." She still couldn't believe the words even though she had said it out aloud. The humor in Candice's face immediately dropped to one of genuine concern and surprise.

Before Emily had started dating Ian, she had shared with Candice her struggles about the idea of a new relationship. Her fear had been real; was she to wait for Tyler, or was she to move on?

Candice was the one who had offered Emily some pearls of wisdom back then, by asking her, *"How much longer are you going to cry over yesterday when God could be giving you something new today?"*

Candice's question often rang in Emily's head on the hard

days. And there were a lot of those days in Emily's life. That piece of advice is what gave Emily the little push to take Ian up on his offer for their first dinner-date. And after one dinner with Ian, Emily knew that if she were ever to love again, it would be with someone like Ian. Perhaps not in the way she had loved Tyler, but in a new and refreshing way.

Candice's voice interrupted her thoughts, asking, "Tyler Hill? Pastor Mike's son?"

Emily rolled her eyes and spoke pointedly. "Yes, Candice, is there any other Tyler I spoke to you about?"

Candice smacked her lips together and put her hand on her hip. "I'm just surprised he's coming back after all these years," she said as she waved her hand in the air. "Even though it's his grandfather's funeral. He comes across as a selfish person."

"He's not selfish." Emily's tone was defensive, and her reply too quick. Candice had picked up on it also. She crossed her arms and gave Emily a stiff look.

"Fine. Then what does Ian think about all of this?"

Emily bit her lip, and her shoulders dropped, defeated. Candice's voice was much more understanding this time. "Em, you need to at least mention it to him. If you don't, it will look like you have something to hide, or even worse, that Ian has something to worry about."

"He doesn't, though." Emily wished her reply could have sounded more confident. It sounded as if she were trying too hard to convince herself of that. She tried rephrasing her comment. "What I mean is," she sighed, "Tyler coming back doesn't change anything with Ian and I. It's just going to be a bit uncomfortable at first."

Candice sniggered, "Emily, these jeans of mine are what you would call *uncomfortable*." She gave Emily's arm a playful whack. "Tyler coming back is a big deal! And what will be uncomfortable is you two seeing each other after a decade with that rock on your hand." She pointed at Emily's ring, her eyes large.

Emily unconsciously covered her left hand with her right one. Candice was right. That was going to be uncomfortable.

Candice continued speaking, saying, "The last time you saw him was at the airport when he had left, right? Before he dumped you over that pathetic text message."

Emily cringed at Candice's remark, and felt the familiar sting of tears make its way to the corner of her eyes. If people put it like *that*, it made her sound crazy for even having all these emotions. She looked at Candice, a guilty expression on her face. "Well, not exactly..."

Candice's eyes grew large. "What do you mean, *not exactly?* You told me that the last time you and Tyler spoke in person was when he was catching his flight out of here. Then he acted like a jerk and completely ghosted you for years after that."

Emily moved her hair over her shoulder and tried to make Candice understand her point. "Yes, that's true. But what he doesn't know, or what everyone doesn't know, is that I did go to find him a year after he had left."

A knowing look came over Candice. She remained quiet, waiting for Emily to go on.

Emily's voice dropped to a sad whisper. "I did find him. At his college," she said while shrugging. "He just doesn't know about it."

The memory pricked Emily as she looked out of the café window, clearly recalling that day. How could she ever forget it?

After being abruptly shut out of his life, Emily had begged her parents to let her go to meet him. She hadn't even told Beth and Pastor Mike that she had a plane ticket to surprise him at his campus. She needed answers from him, and she needed to do something drastic to get them. She wasn't prepared to accept that break-up text message as the final word in their lives.

Arriving at his college campus had been a strange experience. Tyler seemed to be quite popular among the other students, especially with the girls. Emily's plan was to wrap her arms around him, and tell him that she would wait for him as long as he needed her to wait. She had also wanted to ask him one burning question that was eating away at her.

Had he broken up with her because he had blamed her for that night?

A nerdy looking guy eventually pointed Emily to the student parking lot, explaining that Tyler was often there in his free periods with his friends. Emily would never forget the confusion on the guy's face after he had divulged Tyler's whereabouts. He had frowned while asking her, "Are you a friend of his? You don't look like the type he hangs out with."

Emily had found the question strange. What *type* did Tyler hang out with, and what *type* did Emily look like? She didn't bother to ask either of her questions. She had just wanted to find him.

When she had reached the parking lot, she had noticed a group of students hanging around a few vehicles parked towards the end of the lot.

The scene before her looked ominously familiar to the night of the accident. It had made Emily stop in her tracks, her feet glued to the floor. A few drinks were being passed around discreetly from student to student, music was blaring, and right there- in the center of all the attention- was Tyler.

Again.

His arm was draped around a lanky blonde, whose minimal clothing made Emily feel embarrassed for the girl. The entire group looked mildly intoxicated and were oblivious that Emily was standing a few feet away. Tyler's laughter made its way towards her, leaving a dull ache in her heart. He had even sounded different. Emily had planned to make her presence known by walking right up to him.

But at that moment, he had angled the face of the blonde girl towards him. Emily held her breath as she watched him run his hand through the girl's hair while kissing her full on the mouth. Emily's stomach lurched to the point that she thought she was going to be sick right there on the tar plot. Heartbreak was an accurate description of what she had felt at that moment. It was as if someone had squeezed her heart in the palm of their hand, leaving her gasping for air.

The blonde girl had her hands on his shoulders, and when she pulled back, she led him to the backseat of the car. Some of the other students were whistling and hooting in their direction, enjoying the scene that was unfolding.

Emily had not been able to watch any longer. Her stomach clenched in an unbearable knot. At that moment, she had realized that he was not the same person she had known all her life. Since his break-up text, she had spent countless nights crying over him and missing him, yet he was not even thinking about her. His text message had been right. He had moved on. He had chosen a new life, and it was one that didn't involve her or the values, dreams and faith they had once shared.

Emily recalled walking back to her rental car, tears streaming down her face but with a decision in mind. She would nurture her broken heart and would remain silent about what she had witnessed. She would also never pursue Tyler Hill again. It was time to bury the memory of who he was in the same way that they had buried Noah. She knew one thing for sure as she drove out of his college gates that day- it would take a miracle for him to return to her.

Emily remembered the countless nights she had fallen asleep from the mere exhaustion of sobs that wrecked her body. But even as the nights had faded, so did her hopes and dreams for their future together.

Emily felt Candice slide a tissue into her hand, yanking her away from the past memory. Emily dabbed at the unexpected tears quickly, feeling slightly embarrassed for crying in the middle of her coffee shop. If tears still found their way down her face, did it mean her heart was still bruised? Even twelve years later?

One of her customers walked by and gave her a sympathetic smile while dropping some coins in the staff tip-jar. "My condolences Emily. Uncle Bill was a lovely man. We sure will miss him."

Emily nodded sweetly at the lady and exchanged a relieved look with Candice. Candice held Emily's gaze and asked a simple question, her eyebrows raised. "What are you going to say to him when you see him tomorrow?"

Silence hung in the air.

After twelve years, Emily still had no idea what she would say to the young man who had broken her heart in a million pieces.

Four

His flight was on time, and the agitation was mounting.

Tyler shoved his carry on luggage in the overhead compartment and moved towards his window seat. He buckled his seatbelt across his middle and leaned his head back. His stomach growled, but he knew he wouldn't be able to keep any food down if he ate. The nerves wouldn't allow him to. He lifted his gaze to the front of the plane and noticed the flight attendant looking his way, a flirtatious smile on her face. She was attractive. Her blonde hair was in a low bun, and her cherry-colored lipstick glistened as she greeted the embarking passengers and checked their boarding tickets.

Passengers were still making their way through the plane, and Tyler secretly wished they would move faster so that the flight could depart. The waiting was torturous. From his window seat, he watched as people slowly made their way up the staircase onto the plane. His eyes caught a couple who looked like they were in their early thirties. The man had a toddler propped on his hip while his other arm was wrapped around the woman at his side- probably a girlfriend or wife. The woman had a baby-bag slung over her shoulder and their tickets in her hand. She was laughing about something and reached over to pinch her baby's cheek. The baby giggled as the man wiped the gurgling drool from the infant's mouth.

Tyler felt his middle tighten. At thirty-one years old, his life had not turned out like the picture he had once imagined. The pieces of the puzzle of his life were all scattered. Even if he wanted to try and gather them together, he didn't know where to start. Or, what the picture was meant to look like now.

His eyes stayed on the couple until they momentarily faded from his view. Perhaps that would have been him and Emily. They may have been married on a trip to visit their families, probably with a child or two tagging along. The possibilities of what could have been were endless.

Over the years, Tyler had consorted with several women, but none of the relationships were meaningful. He could hardly classify them as relationships either. They were more of one night stands or random drinks at a bar with a colleague when he needed to get his mind off things. Throughout his life, there was only one girl he genuinely cared for. And since he had been incapable of making a relationship last with her, no other woman could come close to taking that place in his life.

The couple with the toddler appeared again, walking down the aisle to find their seats. Tyler secretly hoped they wouldn't take any place near him. The last thing he needed was his short-comings and broken dreams to stare back at him through their picture-perfect faces. He held his breath as they got closer. The man gave him a slight nod as they kept walking towards the back of the plane. Tyler let out the air he was holding in. He wondered if his bitterness towards life and things of the future would ever thaw. He questioned whether he even deserved a chance at having those dreams again after all his actions, and choices.

"Though they are red as crimson, they shall be like wool…"

Tyler's head shot up at the voice. It was the same voice from two nights ago. Tyler swallowed as he looked at the passengers making their way down the aisle of the plane.

It's nobody, you're just hearing things again, he told himself.

He let his mind travel to his parents as he checked the time on his wristwatch. They were probably getting ready for the funeral, also anticipating his arrival in a few hours. Despite the disappointment and the heartache he had inflicted on them over the years, they had always embraced him with a depth of love that he could not understand. Their love for him often made him feel even worse. How could people love someone like that when all that person did was let them down? Those questions added to his reasons for wanting nothing to do with the faith his parents had reared him in. It just didn't make sense to him.

He had spent years of his life hearing stories about God's love, His protection, and His promises. Yet, in one night, Tyler had faced the reality of that faith- it was just a bunch of stories. And he couldn't understand the purpose behind any of it.

If God truly loved His people and if His promises were true, why wasn't Noah saved that night instead of him? What wrong had Noah possibly done to deserve his life being cut short? What mistake did his parents commit that justified losing a good son? What was Emily's sin that her heart had to break?

Tyler ran his hand through his hair, thinking of only one answer to all those questions. He was the common factor in all their lives. He had been the weakest link. He was the cause of the avalanche of pain and brokenness that stemmed from his one night of teenage foolishness.

And now, he was nothing but a hollow man, with nothing to give anyone and with nothing in life to look forward to.

A baby's cries at the back of the plane broke his train of thoughts. He ran his trembling hands down his jeans and leaned his head against the window. He felt his eyelids grow heavy. Dozing off did seem like a better plan than staying awake and fearing the return to his past.

12 years before…

Tyler's head pounded from the hours of studying. He read the last paragraph of his notes, and scribbled some calculations on the side to revise later. He was sitting on the porch at his grandad's house; his legs stretched out comfortably before him with his textbook on his lap.

His grandad's house was his favorite place in the world. The sound of chirping birds and the running stream through the rocks in the backyard soothed his stress. His mother was inside the kitchen, baking her famous apple pie. He could smell the cinnamon from the porch. His father and Noah were busy repainting and fixing the white fence, which was wrapped idyllically around the property.

He could hear their voices and laughter trailing towards him, Noah's especially. Tyler found himself grinning in their direction. When Noah started laughing, he wasn't able to stop easily. It was infectious.

The front porch door swung open, and his grandfather appeared with an extra lemonade in his hand. He grinned at Tyler and bent down, holding it out to him, the moist beads on the glass trickling down.

"You're one clever kid, you know that, my boy?" He motioned towards Tyler's father and Noah, a humorous smile on his face. "You sit here studying while your Dad and brother repair and polish up your future home."

Tyler sipped on his lemonade and let out a chuckle, saying, "They're doing a good job. I've got my eyes on them from here."

His grandfather laughed and took a sip of his drink, letting out a refreshed sound. "You know, Tyler, these kinds of days are the days I will always remember." He motioned around the property. "Being surrounded by family, laughter, and God's goodness. What more could any man ask for?"

Tyler smiled at his grandfather and put his drink to the side of his legs before asking, "But do you ever feel alone here? Like, maybe you should move in with us or get a smaller place?"

His grandfather smiled warmly as he leaned against the porch pillar. His eyes were kind when he said, "My boy, you can never feel alone when you have Jesus." He sipped his drink and looked back at Tyler. "Besides, if I have to move out, there go all your plans to move in and take over this place!"

Tyler let out a laugh and drew his knees up to his chest. "Yeah, I don't think I could ever love another place like this house. I'm glad Noah doesn't feel the same way. The older brother usually gets the best. I would have to fight him for it, if that were the case."

His grandfather flashed him an interesting smile before saying, "In the Bible it's usually the youngest who is uniquely favored."

Tyler frowned. "Really?"

"Oh, yes," his grandfather said, a smile widening across his face as he sipped at his drink. "Moses, David, Jacob, Joseph, Ephraim," he raised his eyebrows and glanced at Tyler humorously before saying, "God always has a special blessing and plan for the youngest one. In time you will find yours and understand that."

Tyler felt moved. He hadn't known that. He needed to read his Bible more to understand those sort of spiritual mysteries.

His grandfather walked closer to him. "Your grandmother and I always hoped that the memories and laughter from inside these walls would continue in our family for generations to come. And that this will always be home for all of you. I'm glad that it's one of your dreams too." He paused. "There is no place in this world that is better than a home."

Tyler loved the sound of that. There was no place better than a home. Their home was really perfect.

A pair of sparrows swooped past them and perched on the railing. His grandfather watched them closely, his voice an eventual whisper as if he were speaking to himself. "And yet, not one of them is forgotten by God."

Tyler frowned, not sure what his grandfather meant by that. His grandfather caught his eye and smiled, picking up on Tyler's confusion. He explained, saying, "The Bible says that not one of these sparrows is forgotten by God. Imagine how much more value we are to Him."

Tyler gazed back at the sparrows and thought about those words. He had never read that in the Bible either. The birds chirped, and Tyler studied them. He was watching them so intently that he hadn't noticed his grandfather looking over at him. When Tyler's eyes met his, his grandfather's voice was tender and profound.

"Always remember that, Tyler. If God can have His eye on that one sparrow," he nodded towards the little one before continuing, "He will never forget you."

Tyler watched him take a sip of his drink as he turned to head back inside. Tyler was amazed at the wisdom and confidence that emanated from his grandfather. All the men in the family were alike in their appreciation for God, His Word, and in their walk with Him. Tyler wished he could be more like each of them. There were still many questions he had, and he struggled with understanding what his purpose was, or what God would use in his life for His Kingdom.

Tyler thought about sharing his concerns and feelings with his family, but he didn't want them to believe he was some kind of skeptic. Besides, it didn't look good for a pastor's son to be asking those kinds of questions. He was meant to have all the answers, wasn't he?

He thought about what his grandfather had said- about the youngest son receiving a unique blessing. Tyler pondered if that was true. If so, he wondered what his special blessing would be, or how long it would be until he received it.

His phone beeped, and he picked it up. The screen light brightened with a notification from his Bible app. It was the daily Bible verse Tyler had scheduled. Since he didn't get the time to read his Bible often, it was one way of being reminded of God's Word daily.

He read the verse on the screen.

Watch and pray, that ye enter not into temptation: the spirit indeed is willing, but the flesh is weak- Matthew 26:41

Tyler's eyes locked on the verse for a little while longer. There were enough temptations to fall into, especially at his age. His friends lived differently to the way he was brought up, to the extent that they often needled him about his values and beliefs. They regularly questioned him about things that he could not an-swer about his own faith.

Tyler looked at the verse and sighed. Being a preacher's son wasn't a walk in the park. He felt held to a higher standard, as if all eyes were on him, eagerly anticipating the moment when he would succumb to temptations and bring shame to his family. The scripture caused his mind to wander.

Why did God allow temptations to be in the world if He didn't want His people to fall into it?

No answer came.

Tyler closed his textbook, slipped his cellphone into his pocket, and made his way towards his father and Noah. He would study the scripture when he had more time.

Noah chuckled as Tyler approached, saying, "Now that this fence is fixed, Dad better get cracking on all the repairs Mom has asked him to fix in our house," he nudged Tyler playfully, "Or else she will be preparing the couch for him tonight."

His father laughed and wiped his brow with the back of his hand. "Noah, it gives me great pleasure to admit that I've only ever slept on the couch once in our twenty-eight years of marriage. A happy wife is a happy life."

"What was it that you did?" Tyler raised his eyebrows and he and Noah shared a curious exchange. They enjoyed teasing their father.

"It's not what *I* did, Tyler. It's what *you* did." His father chuckled and continued, saying, "You had a nightmare when you were about five and crawled into bed with your mother and I. You had a lot of juice to drink before your bedtime," his father raised his eyebrows while stifling a laugh, "and couple that with another nightmare!"

Noah burst out laughing and hit Tyler on his back. "Ty! I recall that phase of your life. I refused to have you sleep in my bed because of that."

Tyler was about to tackle Noah to the ground when a familiar voice interrupted them asking, "What phase of his life?"

Tyler turned to see Emily walking towards them. She had a platter in her hand covered in a silver wrapping. Tyler knew she had been at it again with her pancakes. He prepared his tastebuds for the tasting that would come later.

Emily looked so pretty with her chocolate brown hair hanging around her shoulders in loose curls, and a floral summer dress on, with sneakers. She was not like the other girls who tried too hard to be pretty. She was beauty in simplicity, and her most attractive feature was her wide doe-like eyes. Her eyes were pools of green, and Tyler knew that there were no other eyes in the world as beautiful as hers. Sometimes, he had to pinch himself at the thought that she was his.

"His bed-wetting phase, Em! That's what!" Noah held his sides from his laughter. "You better make sure he's over that phase before you marry him."

Tyler turned on his brother and grappled him to the ground. Even though Noah was five years older and slightly more muscular, Tyler managed to get him in a tight arm lock as they scuffled on the grass. The sound of Emily's laughter rang out, and even their father shook his head at them.

"Break it up, both of you, before one of you gets hurt!" Their mother's voice resounded from the porch and held a serious tone. She shook her head too, clearly frustrated at their antics even now that they were older and should know better. She waved at Emily, a smile lighting up her face as she shouted, "Come join us! The apple pie is ready!"

Tyler loosened his grip on Noah and winked at his brother, saying, "You can thank Mom and her apple pie for saving you today!"

Noah stayed on the ground, breathing heavily with dirt in his hair. He eyed Tyler up and down as he spoke. "You're lucky I spent all of my energy on this fence with Dad, or you wouldn't have stood a chance today. I'll get you later, kid."

Emily ruffled Tyler's hair with her free hand and wrinkled her nose at him. "You want to catch a movie later?"

Tyler dusted his hands together. He knew she wasn't going to be keen on his answer. "I was thinking of stopping by at Ricky's house party for a little bit. It's his birthday, and he did invite me." He took a breath. "I wouldn't want him to think that I ignored the invitation, you know?"

Emily flashed him a concerned look but didn't say anything further. He knew how she felt about Ricky and some of the other guys from their neighborhood and college circles. She motioned at the platter in her hands and spoke, her voice noticeably having dropped a notch.

"Okay, but first, you have to try these pancakes and give me honest feedback. There's cinnamon, pumpkin, banana, and blueberry." Her eyes sparkled. "All your favorites."

Tyler lifted the wrapping from the plate when the smell of fresh pancakes hit him. He broke a piece off from one of them and popped it into his mouth. He let out an *mmm* sound. "Emmy, these are great!"

Emily lifted off her tippy toes, the excitement in her voice back. "Finally! I was at it all morning, getting it perfect just for you. You don't want to see what the kitchen looks like. My mother is not too pleased with me." She paused, her voice curious again. "So, are you sure you don't want to do a movie and dinner, instead of going to this party later?"

Tyler leaned against the fence and looked at his watch on his wrist. A party wouldn't hurt after the hours he had invested in studying. The Bible verse about temptation entered his mind again, and Tyler frowned, brushing it away.

He shaded his eyes from the sun as he looked at Emily, asking, "Why don't you come with me to the party?" He shoved his hands in his pocket. "We can stay a little while and then catch a movie after that. You know Ricky won't let it go if I turn down the invite. He did come to my birthday last year."

Noah stood up from the ground, having caught his breath, and dusted his hands on his jeans. He flashed them both a concerned look. "About Ricky's party," he said, as he shaded his eyes from the suns glare. "I was invited too, but I'm not going. I'm working on the itinerary for that outreach trip tonight. I thought you would want to help, Tyler." He pulled out his phone and typed something before adding, "And on the other hand, I don't think you should care what Ricky thinks about you. You know what his parties are like." His face was disapproving when he spoke again. "The police were called to the last house party he had, remember?"

Tyler felt uncomfortable at his brother's words. Once again, there was a distinct difference between his brother and him. Noah didn't care what people thought of him. But Tyler did care. Ricky would mock him relentlessly, and Tyler was not in the mood for being made a fool in front of the other guys. He had promised Noah he would help on the outreach itinerary, but he just wasn't in the mood for that.

Their father had overheard the entire conversation and finally cleared his throat, giving Tyler a pointed look. "It's not that we don't trust you, Son. But sometimes it's best to avoid those compromising situations." He paused. "But, it's still your choice. You're over eighteen."

Noah let out a disgruntled sound. "Dad, age has nothing to do with it. Tyler should know by now that Ricky and his gang are not the company he should be keeping."

Noah spoke as if Tyler wasn't even standing there. Tyler could hear the disdain dripping from his brother's words as if it was so unbelievable that Tyler was considering going to a simple party. Tyler felt annoyed at him, but he gritted his teeth and kept silent. He also noticed Emily standing by awkwardly as she listened to them.

His father leaned against the fence, his voice kind. "The Bible says we should not refuse instruction, Son. But, like I said," he gave Noah a pointed look before glancing back at Tyler, "It's still your choice, Tyler. I would prefer if you and Emily went for a movie. Or, you could help your brother with the outreach plans as you promised."

Tyler felt a warmth in his cheeks. He understood all their concerns, but he also couldn't help but feel judged, and dictated to. Why did they think they needed to warn him and watch over him like he was a child? Surely, he knew his limits with his friends and could make his own decisions. And so what if he had promised to work on the outreach itinerary? Noah was better at ministry stuff than he was, anyways.

Ricky was once Tyler's best friend. Drinking, smoking, partying, and fooling around with girls wasn't Tyler's idea of a good time. But, he also didn't hold the view that Ricky was an evil person for doing those things either. They were just different. Different people could be friends, couldn't they?

Tyler kept his tone firm, disregarding their opinions and suggestions. "Emily and I won't be there long. We will be in and out. Besides," he shrugged as he turned to Noah, "You will get through the outreach planning much quicker without me."

He saw the disappointment on Noah's face. His brother's lips pinched together as he leaned against the fence.

Emily worried her lower lip and flashed him a concerned look. "Okay, I'll go with you." She looked at Noah and Pastor Mike and shrugged, saying, "I guess we won't stay there long."

Tyler put his arm around her shoulders and led her towards the house, turning his back to his father and brother. He heard Noah mutter something to his father. Tyler kept his voice low when he spoke to Emily.

"I hate when they do that..." He paused before continuing,

"You know? When they act like I'm going to do something dumb." He huffed. "And I can always help Noah some other time!"

She didn't comment until she was at the top of the porch stairs. "Well, maybe they mean well. Maybe they can see into something better than you can." She brushed the side of his face and smiled lovingly. "Any friendship that makes you question your faith, or God, is most likely trouble. Ricky has always been a thorn in your flesh. Why not just cut him off?"

"That's what Jesus would want us to do? Cut people off because they are different than us?" He was caught off guard by his own irritated tone. Emily seemed taken back too. He felt terrible for letting his annoyance with his family and their advice affect his mood towards her.

Tyler ran his hand through his hair. "I'm sorry. That came out wrong." He exhaled slowly. "Let me just grab my jacket, and we can leave."

Emily still looked hurt, but kept her tone light. "A jacket? Are you cold?"

Tyler smiled at her teasingly, trying to lighten the moment. "No. But, my girl will be."

Tyler felt uneasy the entire drive to Ricky's house party. He knew that his father and Noah didn't approve of his decision, but he also wanted to make his own choices. Still, he couldn't shake the peculiar feeling in the pit of his stomach, and he felt too proud to express it either or turn the car around.

The guilt also nibbled at his heart for breaking his promise to his brother.

He'll forgive me, Tyler thought. Noah was a good person in that way.

They neared the house where several cars were lined across the street and parked across Ricky's driveway. Tyler could hear the music even from inside his vehicle. He got off and went around to Emily's door, opening it for her.

She had been quiet since they had left his grandfather's house. But now, her eyes sparkled at him as she got off.

"You were right." Her smile was amusing.

Tyler cocked his head to the side, gazing at her with adoration. After four years together, she still gave him butterflies when she looked at him.

He chuckled. "That's a first!" They shared a laugh as he touched her chin, asking, "Right about what exactly?"

She hugged her arms together. "I need your jacket. It's freezing!"

Tyler let out a single laugh and took his jacket off and wrapped it around her. He helped untuck her hair from the inside of the collar, and watched as it fell around her shoulders.

Their gaze met, and her face grew serious when she spoke. "Tyler, you know you can talk to me about anything, right?" She took his hand. "No matter how scary or crazy it may be, you can always be honest with me."

Tyler hesitated, wondering if he should share his questions

and thoughts about life and faith with her. If there was anyone who would never judge him for having questions, it was Emily. Besides, he never kept secrets from her.

Her green eyes shimmered in the glare of the streetlamp. He took either side of her face with his hands and kissed her. He drew back after a moment and smiled.

"Emmy, there may be many things I have questions about." He watched the uneasiness paint her features, but he continued, keeping his tone even. "But, you are not one of them." He kissed her lightly again, speaking quietly. "You are the only thing I've always been sure about." He ran his thumb down the side of her face and studied her. It was true. She was the only part of his life that he believed in without a doubt. He could live his life without the answers to many things, but he knew he couldn't live his life without her.

Emily bit her bottom lip- something she did when she was concerned. Her face looked as if she were about to say something, but Tyler didn't want to get into it much more than he already had. He pulled her into a hug, and the scent of her vanilla perfume lingered around him. Her arms clung to him, tensely. He hated doing this to her- worrying her and not providing her with the answers she needed. But he didn't want to make his burdens hers. He drew back from her and tucked a strand of her hair behind her ear.

Someone's voice interrupted them. "You two love-birds coming in, or are you guys having your own party outside?"

Tyler and Emily looked over at a friend who was motioning

for them to come in. They shared a chuckle as he led her in by the hand.

The party crowd was a mixture of college students, teenagers from their neighborhood, and a few familiar faces from the church. The music was blasting, and there didn't seem to be any adult supervision around. A few couples had found corners to canoodle in, and another group was throwing back shots near the kitchen. Tyler could smell sweat, smoke, and something sour.

A big sized guy shuffled towards them with a slice of pizza in his hand. He bumped into Emily, and her grip tightened on Tyler so that she wouldn't fall over. Tyler gave the guy a shove as he passed, saying, "Hey man, watch where you're walking." The guy waved him off, disinterested.

Tyler shook his head and looked back at Emily. "You okay?"

She nodded but looked uncomfortable, as she adjusted his jacket around her collar. Tyler felt the familiar stirring inside of him. He leaned in towards her ear so that she would hear him above the noise. "We will stay a little while, and then catch that movie and late dinner. I promise."

Emily nodded quickly, her eyes pensive. Someone called her name, and they both looked over towards a group of her friends from college. Emily waved at them, and Tyler noticed the calm enter her face again. She turned back to Tyler, smiling. "I'll be there with the girls. Come find me when you're ready to leave." She eyed him cautiously. "You promised."

Tyler kissed the back of her hand and smiled, while saying, "Don't forget me, Emmy."

Emily wrinkled her nose and grinned at his statement. For the first time that evening, she seemed herself. Whenever she left his side, Tyler would always tickle her with those four words. The truth was that he enjoyed seeing the bashfulness fall across her face whenever he said it. She squeezed his fingers as she turned to meet her friends. As he watched her go, he heard Ricky's voice shout across the hallway.

"Well, well! It's my buddy, Ty!"

Tyler turned to see Ricky with a group of his friends heading his way. Ricky looked as if he had a few drinks in him already. Tyler knew two of the other guys from the neighborhood, but there were a few faces Tyler had not seen before.

Tyler kept his voice upbeat as he approached Ricky. "Hey man, happy birthday!" He shook his hand and pulled him in for a partial hug. He caught the smell of the alcohol.

Ricky slurred and his eyes were heavy, "I didn't think you would actually come. A party like this must be boring for a pastor's son."

Tyler rolled his eyes. *Here it goes*, he thought.

He touched Ricky's shoulder. "Come on, man. Don't start. Emmy and I wanted to come for a little bit."

Ricky raised his eyebrows and took a swig of the drink in his hand; his beady eyes were darting around the room. "Oh yeah? Your girl's here too?"

Tyler motioned towards Emily, who was sitting on the couch laughing with some of her friends. Ricky wiped his mouth with the back of his hand in a manner that made Tyler squirm.

Ricky turned to his friends, and in a slurring way, asked, "Guys, see that babe with the brown hair?" They followed his pointed finger to Emily's direction as Ricky continued, "That's what you can get if you're a preacher's kid. The good girls."

Tyler felt the muscles in his jaw flex. If Ricky hadn't been a friend of his from the time they were kids, Tyler would have planted his fist right in his face at that moment.

The verse came back to him. *The spirit indeed is willing, but the flesh is weak.*

Tyler knew he needed to leave. Inhaling, he turned to get Emily. Ricky grabbed Tyler's arm playfully while laughing. "Come on, Tyler! I'm just fooling around. Don't be so serious." He took a sip of his drink. "We all know Emily is yours." He winked at the other guys and motioned for them to go outside. He pointed at Tyler, his finger inches from his face. "Stay for a while, and then you can leave."

Tyler gritted his teeth but gave in.

This feeling is probably what that scripture means, he thought.

Everything inside of him was telling him to get Emily and leave the party. But, still, he didn't want Ricky to believe he was rude or a killjoy. He wanted to be Ricky's friend. Perhaps he would be a good influence in Ricky's life. After all, God wouldn't want him to abandon his friends? Would He? Even Jesus sat with sinners, didn't He?

Tyler debated it all within himself. He looked over his shoulder at Emily again as he exited the house. She was showing the girls something on her phone. She seemed like she was enjoying herself. Tyler told himself he would be back for her in a few minutes. After all, he had promised.

Once outside, they headed towards some of the cars parked near the back of the driveway. Tyler heard the sound of bottles clinking. A couple was in the backseat of one of the vehicles, and Tyler had to look away, awkwardness seizing him. One of the shorter guys wearing a neon-colored shirt grabbed a glass bottle and poured the clear liquid into a shot glass and held it out to Tyler.

Tyler shoved his hands in his pocket. "No thanks, I'm cool."

Ricky laughed out loud; his voice mocking. "As long as you don't have this in your hand," Ricky pointed at the glass bottle and continued, "You can never be cool." He took a swig of his bottle and continued. "And you won't be able to hang with us if you don't. You'll have to go back to your Bible study friends."

Tyler pursed his lips and looked over his shoulder back towards the house. It didn't look good if anyone saw the Pastor's son hanging in the shadows with Ricky and his gang whilst they drank. Tyler knew his father wouldn't be pleased. Noah would be disappointed, too. Especially after what both of them had advised him of that afternoon. This was the kind of company they had advised him of avoiding.

"Worried about what your old man would say?" Ricky glared at him, his voice mocking, "About you hanging with the sinners?"

Tyler replied, keeping his voice calm. "Look, Ricky, that's not it. We've been friends for ten years. Give me a break."

Ricky shrugged and leaned across the back of the pickup

truck. He poured another drink into the shot glass and pushed it towards Tyler's chest, saying, "Prove it. You can't celebrate my birthday without a proper drink. What's the big deal? You're not going to hell for one drink." Ricky looked around at the other guys and grinned, "After all, didn't Jesus turn water into wine? I don't know much, but I heard your old man preach that once."

The group roared with laughter.

Tyler felt the eyes of every one of them on him. He didn't know how to answer that. The guys continued laughing and throwing their drinks back. Some of the girls started making their way towards them, one of them batting her eyes at Tyler. Tyler ignored her.

He did wonder what it would feel like to be part of a group of friends and just have a good time on their terms for once. He knew it wouldn't kill him to have one drink. Ricky was right- he wouldn't go to hell for it.

Almost instantly, he remembered Emily's words from earlier that day on the porch steps. "*Any friendship that makes you question your faith or God is most likely trouble.*"

Tyler presented every argument in his head as to why loosening up for one night wouldn't hurt. He wasn't going to become like them. He still believed in God. He would always go to church. Having one drink wouldn't change any of that.

He reached for the drink, even to Ricky's surprise. The moment the drink touched his lips and the tingling sensation made its way down his throat, Tyler felt lighter. He let out a few coughs from the bitterness while the other guys continued guffawing.

Tyler waited for lightning to strike, or for demons to manifest in front of him. But neither came. It was just one innocent drink, and it had been harmless. The guys cheered him on, and Tyler found himself feeling more relaxed than he had felt that entire day. Ricky also seemed to lighten up on the jokes at his expense. The other guys pulled him closer, as if the one drink was a ticket into their circle.

But, as the clock ticked, Tyler couldn't remember how one drink had turned into many more.

Ricky had been right about one thing- Tyler didn't go to hell for that one drink. But, little did he know that once the night was over, and when the morning had broken- he was going to face a different kind of hell.

One that would last the rest of his life.

The ting of the seatbelt sign resounded, and Tyler's eyes flew open. He felt the sweat on his forehead, and he wiped at it quickly. He pinched the bridge of his nose, letting out a breath. He hated being so powerless every time he closed his eyes to sleep. He couldn't free himself from the clutches of his past memories. Falling asleep was like heading into a dark room, uncertain of what he would encounter or whether he would ever find the light switch for an escape.

Everything about the memory of that day was exactly as it had happened twelve years ago. Tyler felt a dull ache within him.

His grandfather's voice, the touch of Emily's lips on his, the taste of that first drink- it all felt real once more.

Tyler pressed his forehead with his fingers. *So many broken promises that night*, he thought.

The flight was now in descent to his dreaded destination. In the seat next to him was an older woman. She looked at him and smiled politely, a book opened in her hands, saying, "You've been out this entire time, Dear! I didn't want to wake you when the snack trolley went by."

Tyler returned the smile and rubbed the corner of his eyes. "It's fine, Ma'am, thank you." In one way, he was happy that he had been asleep when the trolley had passed. His anxiety about returning home may have caused him to order a drink to calm his nerves. He didn't want to do that while he was back.

The woman closed the book on her lap. "So, are you on business or heading home?"

Tyler wanted to answer neither. There was something loving about the woman's disposition, so he responded as politely as possible. "Home." He knew she wouldn't probe further if he just answered the question.

The blonde air hostess walked down the aisle, checking if each row was complying with the descent safety rules. As she passed, she flashed him a smile that lingered a little bit longer than usual. The older woman seemed to have noticed the exchange too. She let out a small laugh and eyed Tyler above her glasses.

"She's a pretty one."

Tyler smiled despite his discomfort. The woman spoke again

through a curious smile. "But, I'm sure a good looking young man like you already has a pretty girl waiting for you back home."

Tyler didn't know if it was a statement or a question. The woman's words felt like a prick to his heart. He looked out of the window as the clouds cleared, revealing the city below him. He clenched his fists as his eyes roamed across the landscape of lakes, buildings, and roads.

He knew two things for sure.

Somewhere down there, below the clouds, was a pretty girl whom he had left behind- a girl whose smile lit his world, and whose green eyes convinced him to believe in the impossible.

And secondly, she would have been foolish to have waited for him.

Five

A sea of faces filled the church.

Everyone whom Michael knew from the congregation and neighborhood had attended. He was moved with gratitude, but not surprised. His father had been special to many.

People shuffled down the aisle serenely, paid their respects to his father at the casket, and made their way toward Beth and him to pass on their condolences. Beth's hand squeezed Michael's now and then. It was always her reminder to him that she was there, thinking about him even while being at his side. He loved that about her.

One of his father's favorite songs was playing through the church. *Because He Lives.* It was a powerful reminder of life. Michael and Beth had attended numerous funerals, and one thing was sure- life was indeed short, and eternity was all that mattered in the end.

Michael checked his watch and glimpsed over his shoulder to

the back of the church. His eyes caught Emily and Ian sitting a few rows behind. They both smiled at him solemnly. Michael nodded at them in a simple greeting before lifting his gaze towards the back doors to scan the crowds for the face he was longing to see.

Beth leaned closer to him and whispered, "He will be here."

Michael swallowed and looked at her, feeling sheepish. He didn't doubt that Tyler would come. He hadn't seen his son in seven months, and he knew that a lot was riding on the days ahead.

A death in their family had caused Tyler to leave. Another death made him return. *What would make him stay?* Michael thought.

Michael put his hand inside his suit pocket and felt the envelope positioned within. He tapped at it carefully. His father's estate attorney had handed the letter to Michael the day before the funeral, explaining what the contents were. Michael felt the lump in his throat grow thicker at the memory. He knew his father had missed Tyler dearly over the years. Still, Michael hadn't expected his father to have written a letter for Tyler before his death. Passing it on to his son was not going to be a small task, or one that he could do in a by-the-way manner. It had to be handled sensitively and at the right time.

Especially because of what was written inside.

Michael looked at the black and white photograph portrait of his father, positioned on an easel in the front of the church. He smiled sadly. Maybe the contents of the letter were his father's way of trying to remind Tyler of who he was, and of the dreams he once had for his life. Or, maybe it was to say goodbye. Michael had not read the letter but he knew his father was a man of wise words. Anything he had written would penetrate a person's heart.

Lord, will his heart soften, or will he run away again? Michael wondered. He hesitated, trying to listen out for any stirring in his heart that may come from scripture or from the Lord's voice to answer him. But instead, he received silence.

If Michael was truly honest with himself, he feared the answer to his own question.

The Father's House.

Tyler stared at the words engraved in a beautiful italic silver print on the cobblestoned wall outside the church. He felt his stomach turn at what the name of the church did to him.

The cars lined the street, and people adorned in black attire were still streaming inside the building. Nobody seemed to have noticed or recognized him as yet. Tyler didn't mind. He knew what was waiting for him once he entered the doors. He anticipated the discreet whispers and disapproving glances directed at him then.

The faint sound of the music from inside the church travelled towards him. The song sounded familiar. He shoved his hands in his pocket and scanned the property again, taking it in. The building looked the same from the last time he had seen it- the same intricate sandstone detail, and the same white window panes. The grass was neatly manicured, and Tyler noticed the bench overlooking the fish pond. He felt his heart miss a beat. Even the bench had not moved from its spot.

It was the spot where he and Emily had shared their first kiss. He remembered the day fondly. They were fifteen. Even then, Tyler knew she was the only girl for him. They had been feeding the fish in the pond, waiting for his parents to finish a meeting inside. The wind played with her hair, and a nervous smile was painted across her face. He had been so conflicted, wondering if he should or shouldn't seize the moment to kiss the friend he had fallen for. He remembered her giving him a curious glance before the side of her mouth titled teasingly as she said, "Yes, you can…"

Tyler remembered the moment vividly. Her cheeks had flushed pink under the summer sun as he planted a simple kiss on her. It had marked the beginning of many special moments with her.

The stirring within his heart brought him back to his senses. Instantly, a pair of sparrows swooped across the walkway and perched on the bench. Tyler felt a flutter inside of him at the sight of the birds. His throat felt constricted.

"And yet, not one of them is forgotten by God." The words came to Tyler instinctively and without invitation. He recalled it as one of the last Bible verses his grandfather had shared with him that fateful day on the porch.

He coughed into his fist, overcome with emotion. *Pull yourself together; it's just a coincidence,* he thought.

If God truly didn't forget a single bird, how had He forgotten their family that night? Tyler gritted his teeth. He wondered where the voice was now that he required some real answers.

He took a deep breath, preparing to enter the one place he had run far away from. And, preparing to face the people he had let down.

Emily was not able to focus that entire morning. She had found it impossible to get through her sleep that night without tossing and turning, thinking about this day. She had created one hundred different scenarios in her head of how their first meeting could go. And not one of those scenarios gave her any peace.

Even as she sat in the fifth row from the front, Emily caught her breath every time someone walked past her in the aisle- knowing that any minute Tyler would be an arms-length away from her. She felt horrible being at Bill's funeral and not being mentally present to mourn or be a comfort to those in need of it. Emily felt like an unraveling ball of wool. She had no idea how she would react, seeing him for the first time since that day in his college parking lot- a day that had toppled her world upside down.

Would he be the one to see her first? Would he end up standing right next to her on the aisle, making it impossible for their eyes to miss each other? Would he avoid her when they did come face to face? All these questions flipped through her head one by one with answers to none of them. Emily tried to calm her reeling thoughts. It didn't do her any good to sit in the church with frustrations burning inside of her. She fiddled with the silver bracelet on her wrist.

"You okay?" Ian's voice interrupted her thoughts, and Emily nodded quickly, letting her hands drop casually to her lap. There were so many secrets hidden in that denial. Ian reached for her hand and clasped it between his, fixing his attention to the front again.

People were slowly making their way towards the casket and circling back to find an empty seat after they shook Pastor Mike's hand or offered Beth a hug. The service hadn't started as yet. Emily checked the time on her watch, noticing that they were running a few minutes behind schedule. She knew Pastor Mike was stalling for the very reason her heart was racing out of control- the one they were waiting for hadn't arrived as yet.

She was still in the midst of her ocean of thoughts when suddenly, a tall figure brushed past her in the aisle. Emily felt her breath catch in her throat, and her stomach tightened. Her heart was beating rapidly, and without realizing it, she felt herself squeezing Ian's hand tighter than usual. Ian was oblivious to it. He covered her hand with his free one and looked down at the order of service pamphlet on his lap.

Emily kept her eyes fixed on the back of the figure. It was Tyler. She knew it. He was tall, broad-shouldered, and his stature despondent. Almost as if he were silently screaming for someone to rescue him. When he reached the casket, he stood still momentarily. The people around him gave him space. Emily saw his hand reach out and touch the edge of it. His head was hung low, and she had the sudden compulsion to go to him and comfort him.

She fought the urge rising within her. When he turned around to head towards his parents, Emily felt the earth below her give way.

Tyler had always been a dashing young man growing up. Emily had been acutely aware of the effect his dark hair, tanned skin, and complimenting brown eyes had on the girls in their circles. She had seen a picture of him pop up on Beth's social media for his birthday a few years after he had left, but the photograph didn't do him any justice as Emily took him in now. He had become strikingly handsome. His face had matured, his jawline more defined.

But he still had the same expression on his face as the moment when the news of his brother's death was delivered to him. A look of defeat and sorrow etched itself deep within his features. Even the way he moved spoke of a lifetime of weariness. It was as if every bit of life was zapped out of him; a dead man walking.

Emily watched both his parents rise to their feet when he approached them. He embraced his father, and they both stayed that way for a long while. Emily wondered if his eyes would fall on her while hugging his father, but they didn't. She was silently grateful that she had the opportunity to take him in first before he saw her. She could see the muscle in his jaw flex as he took a deep breath in, pulling back from his father. Emily watched Beth take the sides of his face with both her hands as she kissed him lovingly on each cheek before rubbing his arm. Beth said something to him, and he flashed her a sad smile and nodded.

Emily felt choked up. She knew what this moment meant for all of them. After twelve years, he was back home. Even if it was against his will.

The moment Tyler took the empty seat next to his mother, Ian leaned in towards her and spoke. His voice was mingled with confusion and curiosity. He had been watching Tyler's exchange with Pastor Mike and Beth the entire time.

"Em, isn't that their son?" He paused. "Your old boyfriend? Tyler?"

Emily felt the heat fill her face. From the corner of her eye, she noticed Ian glance at her. She remained facing forward, hoping her emotions were not written all over her face like an open book. "Yes, that's him."

She noticed a knowing look fall across Ian's features. He leaned back, and his eyes found the back of Tyler's head again.

Ian finally had a face to put to the stories he had heard. He knew that Emily and Tyler had grown up together. He knew that Tyler was her first love. He knew about the accident that caused Tyler to leave and never come back. He also knew that she and Tyler had not kept in touch over the years after their break up. There was nothing further that Ian needed to know. Emily hoped there still wouldn't be anything further to discuss.

She heard him clear his throat softly before leaning towards her, asking, "You okay?" It was the second time he had asked her that question from the morning. But this time, he sounded more concerned.

If the tables were reversed, she would have asked him the same thing too. It was not easy coming face to face with a long lost love. And right now, sitting only a few feet away from the man she had thought about every single day for the last twelve years, Emily knew one thing for sure.

She was definitely not okay.

Tyler felt as if the eyes of every church member were fixed on him. He had noticed the recognition fall across many faces when he walked through the front doors. There was also the occasional whisper and distinct head turns. Some even smiled at him, welcoming him back. Others greeted him with a sympathetic or straightforward nod. A few of his old church friends looked gobsmacked at his arrival, but smiled nonetheless.

People are good at putting on a façade, Tyler thought. He knew what they had said about him after the accident. They had labeled him as rebellious, negligent, a disgrace, reckless, and to blame.

Now that he was sitting next to his parents, many of the strangers were most likely putting the pieces together that he was the long lost son they had heard stories about. He was the *miracle survivor*, as the newspaper article had put it. Tyler scoffed internally at that label.

His grandfather's rich wooden casket glistened in the light. Seeing his grandfather resting inside made Tyler want to break down. His grandfather looked so peaceful and young for his ninety years of age. Tyler wished he could have had one more conversation with him before he passed on. Perhaps Tyler could have told him he was sorry for not being there to take care of him as he had once promised to do. Or, he could have shared one more joke with him to hear his deep and infectious laughter ring out.

It's too late for regrets now, Tyler thought.

The funeral made him uncomfortable. He wondered what his brother's was like. It hadn't been possible for him to attend Noah's funeral since he was still unconscious in a hospital nearby. He couldn't imagine what his parents must have felt on that day, burying their eldest child while worrying about the youngest who was in a coma not far off. He had put them through a nightmare.

The lyrics from the song that was playing in the church made Tyler feel more agitated. He recalled the song playing at his grandad's house on many occasions. He listened to the words again.

Because He lives, I can face tomorrow. Because He lives, all fear is gone. Because I know, He holds the future. And life is worth the living, just because He lives.

Tyler wondered if people really believed all of that. Surely Noah's life was worth living longer than twenty-five years old? And yet, Noah had believed in God. If anyone deserved to die that night, it wasn't Noah. If God truly held the future, then why wasn't Noah sitting here right beside them? Wouldn't the world be a better place with more people like Noah in it and fewer people like him?

All those questions circled in his mind like vultures, making his head spin.

His mother reached for his hand as if she sensed his discomfort. Tyler felt her fingers brush the back of his. He had missed out on so many moments like this over the years. He looked up at the cross at the front of the church. The Bible verse sprawled across the wall caught his eye. It was something new.

And now these three remain: faith, hope and love. But the greatest of these is love...

Tyler studied the words as a memory of some of Noah's last words flashed in his mind again. *"It's very easy to talk about love. Not many people know how to do it."*

Tyler shifted uncomfortably in his seat at the memory, as the last group of people streamed forward to pay their respects. He had to fight the urge not to turn around and take a sweeping glance across the church. He knew that there would be many faces he would recognize after all these years, but he was only interested in the face of one. When he had entered the church, Tyler couldn't help but wonder where she was. But he knew that she was there somewhere, nearer than he thought. A part of him feared turning around if it meant finding her sitting with a husband and child of her own.

Tyler chastised himself. If that was the case, why should it bother him when he was the one who had left her? If she had found someone who loved her and if she had a family by now, he would have to be content knowing that life had worked out well for at least one of them.

Tyler's father got up from his seat, his Bible in his hands, and made his way to the podium on the stage. Tyler had forgotten how great his father looked in that position. There was warmth and deep wisdom that emanated from him, especially when he ministered. Even if one didn't believe in spirituality, his father had a gift of reaching a person's heart with his words and the sound of his voice. Noah had been very much like their father. Tyler noticed his father's sullen expression and the deep lines around his eyes. His hair had flecks of silver in it.

He spoke solemnly. "Firstly, Beth and I would like to extend our appreciation and love to each one of you for being here today. In a time of loss, it is always comforting knowing that there are family and friends who are there to lean on and offer support." He took a breath, his eyes falling to several people. "Days like this remind us that there is a time and season for everything. Being there for one another through the difficult seasons is the test of true friendships and bonds."

Tyler swallowed. Every word that proceeded from his father's mouth felt like arrows to his heart. In a season of loss, he had run in the opposite direction, abandoning them all. Who had been there for his parents when it was a son's duty to have been? Tyler lowered his head, already knowing the answer. He had been so caught up in his grief that he had forgotten theirs.

He cleared his throat as the guilt consumed him. He felt the blood rush through his veins, and his ears were on fire.

His father paused momentarily and smiled at everyone. "My father lived an abundant life. Those of you who knew him can confirm that there was rarely a day when he didn't have a smile on his face or an encouraging word to pass on." His eyes found Tyler's mother, and he smiled. "His home was just as open as his heart was to every one of us. He was that kind of man. He was a man who recognized the Lord's hand in everything."

A beautiful silence hung in the air as if people were reminiscing at their memories with Bill. Tyler recalled the words his grandfather had once said to him.

"*There is no place in this world that is better than a home.*"

Tyler tried to stifle the memory, afraid of what the words would do to him. Even though he was back in his hometown, his heart had not experienced the feeling of home in a long time.

His father continued speaking. "Over the years, my father would say many profound things. But there was always something he said which I found such beauty in."

Tyler's mother dabbed at the tears running down her face. He reached out and squeezed her hand gently whilst shifting his gaze back to his father, awaiting his words. His grandfather had said many wise things throughout his life. Tyler wasn't sure which words of wisdom his father would share with everyone.

"My father said that to have peace, one must know the Prince of Peace."

Tyler felt as if someone had punched him in the gut. He inhaled sharply. Those were the exact words he had heard two nights ago when the nightmare of the accident had woken him. At the time, he could have sworn someone was in the room with him, speaking those very same words. But now it made sense. It was something his grandfather had shared at some point.

Tyler shifted awkwardly in his seat. He had only been in the church a short while, and he was already feeling smothered. He felt targeted from all directions. His body felt as if it was sinking into a chasm. It was similar to the moments in the hospital when he had been fighting to regain consciousness.

His father continued speaking. "He always said that this life on earth is just a drop in the ocean compared to eternity, and that we are all just passing through until we finally enter rest in our true home." He paused and continued, his voice cracking. "For those of you who don't know this… several years ago, we lost our eldest son quite tragically. Noah."

The heat consumed Tyler's body, and he cringed. He wanted to reach for his tie and loosen it around his neck before he passed out. Racing to the door would have been better, but his mother's hand over his reminded him that he was stuck there, in the front row, forced to face every word head-on.

At the drop of Noah's name, Tyler felt like every eye in the church was drilling holes into the back of his head. They all knew the reason why Noah wasn't there.

Breathe, he told himself. Why would his father bring Noah into this? Was it to make him feel accountable in the presence of so many people? Was his punishment over the years not enough?

His father's voice was gentle. "Today, I have peace knowing that when Dad arrived at the gates of Heaven, both my mother and Noah were there to usher him into the kingdom." He smiled and looked at the casket. "It must have been a real celebration when they entered the true Father's House." His father ran his hand over the Bible and looked across the room, his eyes soft as he spoke, saying, "Even in dark times, we should remember that there is nothing that can separate us from the love of God. And we are all one step closer to reuniting with them if we, too, choose the Prince of Peace."

Tyler held his breath as his father's voice trailed off. The words were pointed directly at him. He was the only hypocrite sitting in the church who had turned away from God and his belief. Tyler's mother wiped at a tear and nodded. A few *Amens* resounded around the church, each affirmation making Tyler feel smaller and smaller.

Tyler's parents had never spoken to him about their views on his decisions over the years. But after hearing his father's message, Tyler realized where they both stood. They believed he was on a journey with a one-way ticket straight for a lost eternity for rejecting God and His Word. Tyler sighed and lowered his head.

What they didn't realize was that he didn't need to wait for eternity to be lost. He was lost even now. Nothing made sense to him. He had to do whatever he could to drown out the truth of his life and to live with the consequences of all his actions.

Despite the verse that hung on the wall of the church about faith, hope, and love, Tyler knew that there was something else nobody was mentioning.

There was the *truth* too. The truth had been the weight he was carrying for twelve years since that night. The truth, was that he was the last person on earth who deserved fulfillment or peace. After all, he had been responsible for robbing the life of his own brother, and bringing brokenness to the doorsteps of the lives of those he loved.

Tyler looked up at the cross with one question in his mind. What kind of God would forget his wrongs and give someone like him healing and peace for the future?

Six

Even after the church service had come to an end, Emily was still nowhere to be seen.

Groups of people pressed together, trying to exit the church. Latecomers nudged their way forward to pass their condolences to Tyler and his parents. There were familiar faces everywhere he turned, except for hers.

He wondered what she looked like, what she was thinking, and whether she would even speak to him after all these years. A thought crossed his mind that she had seen him and decided to leave early to avoid a confrontation. He wouldn't have blamed her if that were the case. He had ended their relationship in such a despicable manner, basically slamming the door of his heart right in her face, and never having explained why.

The gathering at the cemetery was a smaller group of people; those who had not attended the church service and those who were the closest friends and family wanting to bid their final goodbyes to Bill. Tyler stood at the front of the plot with his parents as the casket lowered into the ground. The wind rustled the leaves across the grassy banks. He pulled the coat of his suit together and reluctantly bowed his head through the final prayer.

The cemetery brought back feelings of despair. He had been there once before, twelve years ago- on the day when he was leaving for a new city. A familiar memory from that day filtered into his mind even as he watched the casket disappear beneath him. It was a conversation with a stranger who had caught him off guard while he was at Noah's grave, saying goodbye. A grave-keeper, Tyler remembered.

The man had said something to Tyler about floods and rainbows. Tyler raised his eyes and scanned the graves in the distance. His brother's plot was somewhere there, under a large tree. He promised himself he would never go back to visit it. He just couldn't imagine his brother in the ground like that. But he did wonder whether that grave-keeper was still around. Gabe, his name had been.

When the service and burial were over, Tyler moved aside as several people came forward with flowers and candles to lay around the plot. Suddenly, the crowd parted, and his eyes fell on her. His breath caught in his throat.

Emily. His Emmy.

Every voice around him drowned out in an instant, and he felt as if time stood still. He heard nothing else except the sound of his breathing and the faint rustling of leaves around his shoes. From where he was standing, Tyler recognized the same girl he had known twelve years ago- his best friend, and the one he had promised and planned to spend his life with.

She was poised, her face downcast. A simple black dress framed her form perfectly. Her dark hair hung in soft, loose waves around her shoulders; the same way it had always done. She looked like a young Jennifer Connelly.

Now and then, the breeze would move her hair around her eye, and she would slowly tuck it behind her ear- something he recalled often doing for her. Tyler noticed the man standing next to her. The man's hand was carefully resting on the small of her back. Tyler felt a pang of envy, realizing the man was with her. It was bizarre seeing Emily with someone else. He wondered if the man was her husband, or a boyfriend.

Over the years, he had never asked his parents about her, and neither did they offer up any information. He was in the dark about what had come of her life. Tyler felt his palms grow damp, and he pressed them against his pants. He couldn't just ignore her or pretend that he had not seen her. But what would he say to her? How would he ever ask for her forgiveness for what he had done? Was she even interested in an apology after all these years?

As he remained fixed on her, her eyes lifted from the ground and locked on his. A wave of emotions took hold of his heart, making him feel raw and exposed. He wasn't expecting her gaze to move him so deeply, but he was helpless to it.

She was more beautiful than he remembered. But something about her was different. Her eyes had grown dull. She was staring coldly back at him, as if seeing him didn't matter to her at all.

Tyler felt a sting within him, and he shifted uncomfortably in his position. He needed to speak to her.

Before realizing it, his feet responded to the familiar magnetic pull towards her. It was unavoidable; he was going to come face to face with the girl he had loved since he was fifteen years old.

Seeing him for the first time, after a decade, was unlike anything she had imagined it would be. Emily had not been ready for it. Ian's attentive gaze made her more nervous. She hoped that she wouldn't slip up in a facial expression or tone of voice that would give away her feelings.

But at the cemetery, Emily couldn't run or hide from the inevitable. No amount of crowds or trees could disguise her. If she didn't speak to him, it would look worse. She had watched him the entire time until her attention diverted to some of the parents of her youth group. But when she had finally looked up again to find him, his eyes had already located her.

They were narrowed in on her, like a laser on its target.

Their eyes connected for what felt like a lifetime. With one glance, memories of adventurous summers, fun church socials, bicycle rides through the park, and deep conversations under the moonlight played back like a picture on the big screen.

Emily wondered if her eyes would give away what her lips could never say.

It was difficult to discern his thoughts or feelings. Before she could take a deep breath to prepare herself, he was already walking towards her. Emily cleared her throat to find her voice so that it would not crack when the time came to speak. She needed to be strong- to show him that he had not hurt her as much as he honestly had.

As he approached, she realized how much taller he was than she last remembered. Ian was standing right next to her, his hand on her back.

The moment she had been waiting for and wondering about over the years was finally at hand. After every broken promise, many sleepless nights and plenty of unanswered questions, Tyler Hill was in front of her.

"Emily..." His voice was polite, but husky. The sound of her name on his lips hadn't changed. It still sounded as sweet as honey. Emily didn't know if he was intending to put his hand out to shake hers or move forward for the embrace. She decided to make the choice easier by keeping her hands folded rigidly in front of her. She wasn't ready to touch him or have his arms around her. She couldn't trust herself around him.

He smiled in a somewhat conflicted manner, shoving his hands in his pockets, before saying, "It's good to see you."

Emily flashed a forced smile his way. "You too. I'm sorry about Uncle Bill." Her tone sounded standoffish. She was sorry about a lot of things, but that was all she could muster at that moment.

Ian cleared his throat next to her and put his hand forward to introduce himself, something she had neglected to do. "My condolences for your grandfather. I'm Ian." He looked at Emily and then back at Tyler. "We haven't met before."

Emily couldn't help but notice Ian's firm handshake still in place nor the muscle in Tyler's jaw flex when he returned the greeting. Tyler kept his face polite through the exchange. "Thank you. It's nice to meet you." He paused and continued. "I'm Tyler, by the way."

Ian knows very well who you are, Emily thought. An awkward silence followed, and Emily suddenly realized that she didn't know what to say or ask next. All her prepared speeches and scenarios had disappeared in the wind.

Ian seemed to pick up on the tension, so he took the lead to speak instead. "So, Tyler, how long are you in town for?"

Emily didn't want to read too much into Ian's question, but she was curious why he asked such a thing. Was he wondering how long Tyler was going to be around her, or was he just making small-talk?

Tyler shoved his hands in his pocket, and his eyes glanced at Emily with an unblinking intensity. He quickly focused back on Ian, replying, "A couple of days. I haven't decided as yet."

"Well, I'm sure everyone is looking forward to having you around for a while," Ian shoved his hands in his pocket before continuing, "I'm actually heading out of town for a business conference. It would have been nice to hang out."

Emily wanted to interject and say no, it wouldn't be nice for her. Hanging out with the man she had dreamed of marrying and the man whom she was going to marry instead didn't sound nice at all. She chose to keep that thought to herself.

It was as if she was invisible, just standing there listening to the polite exchanges between both men. With both of them standing in front of her, Emily realized how different they were. Ian was blonde with a gentleness and confidence in his voice. Tyler was dark-haired, and his face had an intensity to it. His voice was also guarded whenever he spoke. The men were poles apart. And she was now smack-bang in the middle.

Tyler nodded. "It would have been nice. But I hope you have a safe trip. I'll probably be gone by the time you get back." He stuck his hand out at Ian, saying, "It was nice meeting you." Tyler looked back at her, and his gaze lingered a second longer than it should have. "It was nice seeing you again, Emmy."

Emily recognized the thickness in his voice. She realized that this moment was as awkward for him as it was for her. His voice held an apologetic tone. Emily wondered why. He was the one who had hurt her, not the other way around. She wondered if seeing Ian at her side caused him to feel something he wasn't expecting. If he was, Emily thought that he deserved it. Did he really think that she would have been sitting around, waiting for him to come to his senses? Or, that he had damaged her so deeply that she would never have moved on?

She kept her voice as natural as possible, saying, "Yes, you too, Tyler."

He turned and walked off towards his parents, who were still standing at the grave plot, speaking to one another. Emily watched Pastor Mike put his hand on Tyler's back when he reached them, and they shared a few words. Beth looked over at Emily, the emotion on her face reflecting her understanding of the situation. Emily could have used a hug from her at that moment.

"Emmy…" Ian's voice interrupted her swirling thoughts.

She looked at Ian and noticed his eyes were still focused on Tyler. There was a strange look in Ian's eyes; one Emily had not seen before.

Ian angled his body towards her and kept his tone flat when he spoke, saying, "*Emmy*. So, that's what he called you…"

Emily felt as if the ground had opened. She hadn't even realized that Tyler had just given away a secret of hers. Emily had never told Ian why she had named the coffee shop *Emmy's*. She never believed it would come up. And now, there was no need to explain further. Ian knew.

Emily inhaled, relieving some of the tightness in her chest. Tyler had not even been around for more than a few hours, and already, she felt as if everything was caving in.

Seven

Tyler stood in the doorway of Noah's room and scoured the inside. His parents had converted the room into a spare bedroom. There was nothing familiar about it.

Noah once had numerous trophies and awards spread out across the shelves and walls. Now, simple paintings hung neatly in those places. Noah's desk and office lamp near the window had also been replaced by a sky blue tuxedo style sofa. The bed was much larger too.

The changes made Tyler uncomfortable; as if there was no trace of Noah ever having lived there. He wondered how long it had taken before his parents had packed Noah's things in boxes. Tyler dropped his luggage in the corner of the room and stepped in.

He recalled the hours they had spent playing board games and studying there. The hairs on the back of his neck started to rise. Although the interior looked different, the memories of their childhood remained etched in his mind. So was the sound of their laughter and roughhousing within its four walls.

A photo frame positioned neatly on a bookshelf caught his eye. Tyler walked towards it and picked it up. It was a photograph of Noah and him at their grandfather's house. It was the only thing belonging to Noah that his parents hadn't removed from the room.

In the photograph, Tyler and Noah were sitting on the porch steps in matching blue stripe T-shirt's. Tyler must have been about six years old, and Noah around eleven. Tyler remembered the day crystal clearly. His parents were busy at a marriage counseling seminar. Tyler and Noah had been packed off to their grandad's house to spend the weekend climbing trees, eating junk food, and watching movies past their bedtime. The memory brought a smile to his face. It had been one of the best days of his childhood.

The sound of his father's throat clearing made Tyler spin around. He quickly put the frame back where it belonged. His father leaned against the door, an understanding look on his face as he said, "If you're not comfortable in here, we can re-arrange your old room to accommodate you." His father paused before shrugging. "Your room had better lighting for my office space. We would just need to get a bed in there if you really want to move."

Tyler thought about the offer. It did feel strange to sleep in Noah's room, but he didn't want to be petty. He was not planning to stay for long in any event.

His father's voice interrupted his thoughts again. "Or, your grandfather's house is available if you want your own space. You always preferred being there, anyways."

Tyler noticed something strange flash over his father's face when he mentioned Bill's house. The house would be empty now that his grandfather was gone. Emptiness was not how Tyler remembered that place. It had always been a home filled with bellowing laughter and significant moments.

Tyler frowned at his father's comment, asking, "Why would I be uncomfortable here?" He took a step away from the bookshelf and shrugged in a slack manner, adding quietly, "You and Mom have changed everything. I can barely recognize it."

His father sensed his sarcasm. He walked in and looked around, as if it were his first time taking the room in.

His lips pursed before explaining to Tyler, "It took a long time before we were able to do so. We thought Noah would have approved if we turned it into a spare bedroom for anyone needing a place to crash for a night or two." His father looked at the photo on the shelf, adding, "We've met some great kids over the years from doing that."

Tyler didn't know what to say. He almost felt guilty for being quick in judging his parents motives.

His father's voice dropped a notch. "We run a youth program at church in Noah's honor. A lot of the kids who have troubled lives and just need someone to talk to or guide them through their problems have joined. It's really amazing."

Tyler swallowed the knot in his throat and sat down on the bed. "Yeah, Noah would have approved of that. He always had ideas to start a youth group."

His father smiled and put his hand on Tyler's back. "Well, from what I recall, the idea came from the both of you."

The reminder stirred an uneasiness in him. Noah and Tyler had bounced ideas off of one another to run a youth group at the church that would help teenagers navigate life with faith-filled values. But that was before anyone realized that Tyler needed help of his own in that department.

His father cleared his throat, saying, "Maybe you could check it out while you are here. The kids may like that."

Instead of saying what he truly felt about that suggestion, Tyler chose to remain silent. What good would he be to any youngster? He was the worst example who had fallen prey to destructive influences in life. He would be a hypocrite to warn them of life's obstacles and curveballs.

His father moved forward, taking the spot on the bed next to Tyler, his hand never leaving Tyler's back. "Everyone at church was happy to see you today."

Tyler gritted his teeth. That's not what he had sensed. He kept his voice polite as he responded, saying, "They were just being sympathetic, given the circumstances."

"Even Emily?" His father's question caught Tyler off guard. His father had seen him talking to Emily and Ian at the cemetery. He was probably fishing for some feedback of their long-awaited reunion.

Tyler nodded slowly. "It was nice seeing her. She hasn't changed that much."

"Oh, she has, Tyler." His father fiddled with a stray strand of cotton on the bedsheet before finding Tyler's eyes. Tyler didn't want to ask him what he meant by that, because he knew he wouldn't like the answer. Emily's appearance may have looked the same, but what he had done to her heart had changed her attitude.

She was more guarded and stoic. Tyler couldn't forget how cold her eyes were when she had first looked at him. He hated to admit it, but it had hurt.

His father spoke sincerely. "I can imagine it must have been difficult for her to have seen you after all these years. It wasn't easy on her when you left." He paused and kept his tone light. "But knowing Emily, she would have been happy to have seen you. Even if she didn't say it."

Tyler looked to the outside of the window, a question bubbling within him.

"Is she married to Ian?" The question had plagued him since leaving the cemetery. He knew the answer wasn't going to change anything, but he just wanted to know how her life had turned out after he had left. Or, maybe, he secretly itched to know how long it had taken before she moved on from loving him.

A girl like Emily wasn't going to remain single for very long.

His father stood up from the bed and walked to the window. "No, but they are engaged. The wedding is in a few months. Her parents moved away from town a few years back, so your Mom has helped her out a lot with the wedding plans. They've asked me to do the ceremony."

Tyler felt an odd sensation creep up within him. Both his parents were involved in helping Emily's wedding plans, something that would have ordinarily been theirs, if life had gone as intended. Tyler felt the muscle in his jaw flex. Everything was so messed up. He had messed everything up.

He kept his tone even. "Did she know I was coming?"

An amused smile found his father's face. "Your mother said I had mentioned it in her presence, unknowingly." He shrugged. "Regardless, I'm sure she knew you would be coming back home at some point."

Tyler inhaled, and without realizing it, his words were out and grating. "I'm not *back home,* Dad."

He saw the troubled look brew beneath his father's eyes. Tyler broke his gaze so that he wouldn't have to look at him. He let his eyes fall on the photograph with Noah again. He worked hard to soften his tone this time. He didn't want to hurt his father with his callous response, but he needed to speak the truth.

"I don't know if I would have come back if it wasn't for the funeral," he said.

His father crossed his arms as his gaze dropped to the floor. He looked as if he was about to say something when the sound of footsteps drew nearer. Tyler saw his mother make her way around the corner. As she entered the room, her eyes darted between both of them, sensing the uneasy tension.

She held a set of keys in her hands as she took a step in, asking, "Did something happen?" Her voice was concerned.

Tyler faked a smile as his father answered her. "No, nothing, Love. Tyler and I were just talking about Emily and Ian."

His mother raised her eyebrows. "Oh, well speaking of Emily…" She tossed the set of keys at Tyler, who instinctively grabbed it in the air, as she continued, "Can you drop those off for her at the café on the corner of Crescent and Sixth by the morning?"

Tyler stood up and held the keys back towards his mother, shaking his head as he replied, "Mom, I don't think that's a good idea…"

"Tyler," His mother's voice held no room for negotiation. He felt as if he were seventeen again. Something about it made him want to smile. His mother pushed on relentlessly. "I only asked you to drop off keys at a café, not to move back home." She gave him a scathing look. "And we all know that one of those things would be much easier for you to do right now."

Tyler felt rueful, and noticed the humor fall across his father's face. His mother was right.

Her first request wasn't as impossible as the second.

Eight

12 years before...

Emily's heart rate doubled.

Something about Tyler's demeanor didn't settle well with her. From Ricky's doorway, Emily noticed the drink in Tyler's hand, even as he laughed uncontrollably. Another guy had his arm slung around Tyler's neck, also doubling over with laughter. She felt a pit in her stomach. He had promised that they would leave the party, but time had escaped the both of them.

She made her way down the pathway to the spot where the group was socializing. Some of the guys were stacking empty glass bottles in a tower at the end of the driveway, and were taking turns in knocking it down with a can or a stone, shattering the glass into pieces across the pavement. The sound of the shattering glass made her cringe as she overstepped it. She knew it was only a matter of time before the neighbors called the police, or before someone got seriously injured.

When she approached the group, a choir of whistles and cat-calls were directed her way. Some of the other girls gave her a snobbish scowl as she brushed past them. Emily flashed Ricky an infuriated look as she made her way to Tyler. She tugged on his arm, turning him around to face her. That's when she saw his face, and her fears were realized.

He had been drinking. His cheeks were flushed, as if he had been running a marathon. His eyes held a glazed shimmer, and his smile was too enthusiastic.

Emily spoke to him firmly, saying, "Tyler, lets go."

His balance was slightly off as he draped his arm around her neck. She caught the smell of the alcohol on his breath, and she had to turn her face away. The smell alone told her that he had more than one drink in him. Questions started to swarm through her mind, but it was neither the time nor place to get into it with him. She knew he had been acting strangely that day, but she had never prepared herself for this out of character encounter. Especially not after all their words of advice and warnings. She already feared what his family were going to say.

When he spoke, his words were slurry. "Emmy, I'm not ready to go yet." He sounded like a petulant child, and it annoyed her.

She tightened her grip on his arm, speaking through gritted teeth, saying, "It's past eleven, Tyler. Our parents are going to wonder why we aren't back as yet. We told them we wouldn't be here long."

Before Tyler could respond, Ricky chortled and waved his

hand in their direction. "Hey Tyler, you gonna let her tell you to stop having some fun? Are you both late for a family Bible study?"

The others burst out in laughter, high-fiving each other as if Ricky were a comedian. Emily had the urge to turn around and give them all a piece of her mind, but she knew it would be pointless. She would have more feedback from a brick wall than a group of drunken boys. Tyler was roaring with laughter, even though the joke was an insult directed at him and their faith. When she tried to pull him towards her to leave with her, he broke her grip from his arm. His rough reaction caused her to miss her step, and almost lose her balance.

This time he glared at her, his voice a notch louder. "Emily, just go home!" The over-enthusiastic grin that he had on his face earlier was wiped off and replaced with an angry scowl. He was acting as if she was embarrassing him in front of his new pals. Fresh tears welled up in Emily's eyes, and she felt humiliated. The other girls were sneering in the corner.

"Tyler, please let's leave. Give me your car keys, I'll drive us," she pleaded.

He stumbled to the side of the driveway and plonked himself down, taking another swig from the glass he was holding onto firmly. He wiped his mouth with the back of his hand. Emily took a step forward towards him just as he met her eyes again.

He spoke more calmly this time. "Emmy, I said go home. I'm not leaving."

The fight left her at that moment. Emily knew she was never going to be successful in dragging him out in that condition. Tyler was not one to act that way or even speak to her in that manner. A lump formed in her throat as she turned around to leave. She noticed some of the other girls mocking her over their shoulders. Emily knew that if she wasn't able to knock some sense into him and take him home, someone else would be able to.

She walked off, defeated, and with tears spilling down her face. She pulled out her phone and scrolled down her contacts. She hesitated before dialing, and wondered if her decision would open up a can of worms in his family. The last thing she wanted to do was get Tyler in trouble. But she couldn't ignore the compromising position he was in- intoxicated, with his car keys on him.

So many things could go wrong, and she could never forgive herself if it did. Whatever he was dealing with, she would help him through it when the evening was over and when he was in the right frame of mind.

She gnawed at her bottom lip, not knowing what to do. She looked over at Tyler again and watched him roar with laughter with his new group of friends. A girl was hanging around him, too close for Emily's comfort. He hadn't even watched her leave, and he didn't seem to care that he had left her to find her way home alone.

Emily wiped at the tears on her face and pressed the call icon on the screen.

The phone rang and rang until finally, Noah answered.

Tyler's head was swimming, and he felt a wave of nausea rise in his stomach. He couldn't remember how many drinks he had thrown back. Or even why. He held the lower part of his abdomen and hurled into the bushes on the side of Ricky's driveway. He could hear the other guys bellowing with laughter behind him.

Ricky walked over to him and hit his back, asking humorously, "You alright, man? For someone who has never had a drink before, you really went all out tonight."

One of the other guys laughed and chimed in, saying, "Yeah, he really showed us! You said he would be a hard one to crack!"

Tyler wiped his mouth and sat down on the side of the driveway, ignoring them both. He felt physically sick, and his head was pounding. He looked at the time through his blurred vision and could barely make out where the needles were pointing. It appeared to be past midnight.

He thought about Emily. He wondered if she would ever forgive him for how he had acted earlier. He had a lot to explain and make up for in the morning. As he was about to fall back on the cool pavement, he heard a familiar voice shout at him.

"Tyler, get up!"

Tyler looked up from where he was sitting and saw Noah's face, looking down at him. Disappointment was etched across his brother's features.

Tyler frowned at him, asking, "Noah, what are you doing here?" Some of his words felt difficult to say. He tried to get up and must have stumbled back because Noah grabbed his arm to support him. Tyler heard Ricky say something to Noah, who then fired a cheeky response back. To Tyler, Noah's words sounded muffled. But, he could hear his brother's tone and it wasn't pretty.

Noah fumbled inside Tyler's jean pockets until he located the car keys. Before Tyler knew it, Noah had bundled him into the passenger seat of the car. He heard the driver's side door slam with force as Noah got in. They pulled onto the road quickly, tires screeching.

"Tyler, what made you do something like this?" Noah took a sharp right turn, which made Tyler want to hurl again. His brother's voice sounded exhausted. "Emily called me in a frantic state. You've got a lot to explain tomorrow. You better hope Mom and Dad don't wake up and see you enter the house in this state. That's if the smell doesn't wake them first."

The pounding in Tyler's head wouldn't stop. It got worse as Noah spoke, each syllable spoken like a hammer to his brain. Tyler couldn't understand how others were able to drink and party most of the night without feeling this terrible. Surely, they didn't enjoy this?

Tyler ran his hand through his hair and let out a defiant chuckle. "I didn't rob a bank or kill anyone, Noah. We were just having some fun."

"*Fun?*" Noah's voice was louder, clearly not pleased with Tyler's sarcastic response. "So, this is fun for you? It's fun that Emily had to get a cab and go home alone at this hour? It's fun that I had to leave home in the middle of the night without even telling Mom and Dad?" Noah let out a frustrated-sounding sigh. "Since when did you become like Ricky and his friends? We thought you knew better."

The question irritated Tyler. He shot his brother a hard look, asking, "What's wrong with Ricky and his friends? Just because they loosen up once in a while doesn't make them bad people, you know? You may actually enjoy it too."

The road lights were out as Noah turned onto the highway. It was darker than usual. Noah decreased his speed. The motion of the car still made Tyler feel like he was on a rollercoaster- the feeling when you idle at the highest point before dropping at a rapid speed.

Tyler leaned forward, his hand across his stomach. "Can you pull over real quick?"

Noah shot him an annoyed look and pulled the car to the side. Tyler opened the door, and just about managed to lean out when everything inside him came spilling out. After a few moments of dry heaving and chest spasms, Tyler felt a little bit better. The muscles in his chest relaxed. He slowly moved onto his seat again and leaned his head back, wiping the back of his hand across his mouth.

Noah grabbed the bottled water from the center compartment and shoved it into Tyler's chest, sarcastically responding, "Yeah, I can see what *fun* I'm missing out on."

A silence followed for a while as they continued to drive. Tyler leaned his head against the cold window. He agreed with Noah- he hoped his parents weren't going to be up to see him walk in like that. He didn't need another lecture about right and wrong. He needed water and sleep.

Noah broke the tension, his voice calmer. "Listen, kid, I understand there are many challenges and temptations when you are young. Nobody is immune to them." Tyler suddenly thought back to the Bible verse he had received on his phone earlier that day about temptations. He didn't want to comment on it.

Noah continued. "But, every decision you make has consequences. It's the small foxes that ruin the vine, remember?"

Tyler did remember. It was a message his father once preached, about how people always focused on the sins that they considered to be big. Yet, it was usually the little temptations and small weaknesses that creep in to ruin a person's life and purpose.

Noah stopped at a traffic light as it went from yellow to red and angled his position to face Tyler, his one hand still on the steering wheel. His face was more relaxed this time when he spoke. "All I'm saying is that you need to be wise in life. When there is a great purpose on your life, the enemy will try and look for an opening to come in and destroy you. Don't give in." He took a breath. "Think about it. What did tonight achieve? You became someone you aren't. You broke a promise to me. You hurt the girl you love and who loves you. If Mom or Dad found out about this, they would be so disappointed. And right now, you can't tell me you feel great after this night."

Tyler let each word sink in. He didn't want to admit it, but Noah was right in a way. It made him think back to the part in that Bible verse, which said, *The spirit is willing, but the flesh is weak.*

Maybe that verse was God's way of preparing him or warning him about tonight. He didn't understand it then, but what Noah was saying was precisely that. The spirit is willing to make the right choices, but the flesh is easily influenced and needs to be overcome.

Tyler looked out the window at the passing cars. The streets were still busy even though it was the first hours of the morning. His voice was despondent as he looked at his brother and said, "I'm not as strong as you are, Noah." He let out a sigh. "Unlike me, you know without a doubt who you are and what your purpose is. I have so many questions about our faith and all of God's rules."

Noah frowned, his tone dropping. "Is that how you see it? His Rules?"

Tyler threw his hand in the air. "What else is it then? I'm always hearing don't do this, don't do that, stay away from this, flee from that…" He sucked in a breath. "Why does God put us in this world and then make it so difficult to get through it? It's as if He's testing us and is just waiting for us to slip up."

Tyler noticed the empathy on Noah's face. His brother's voice softened as he angled towards Tyler. "Okay let me ask you this," he paused before continuing, "In your relationship with Emily, what are some of the things that you know could hurt her, and would prevent you both from having a future together?"

Tyler studied his brother, uncertain what Emily or their relationship had to do with the conversation about God.

He answered despite his confusion, saying, "So many things. Like lying to her, deceiving her, cheating on her, criticizing her," he waved his hand, "I could keep going."

Noah nodded as if he were expecting that answer from him. "Then, why don't you do any of those things?"

Tyler looked at him, blankly. "Because I love her, and she means everything to me. It would break her heart if I did. I would never want to hurt her."

Noah smiled, clearly making his point. "Exactly, kid. When you are in a relationship with the Lord, you want to live a pleasing life so that you don't grieve His heart. And when you know His Word, you become more familiar with His desires for your life. It's not a bunch of rules. It's a blueprint to a life of purpose and peace, if you want it. When you've truly encountered who He is, it's easy to follow Him, and give up all the foolishness this life is offering."

The words started to unravel something in Tyler.

Noah let out a single laugh and fisted Tyler's shoulder playfully. "The Bible says if we love Him, we will do what He says. It's very easy to talk about love. Not many people know how to do it." Noah took a breath. "There's so much more out there than drinking, partying, and…" he chuckled mockingly, "What were the words you used? *Loosening up?*"

Tyler found himself smiling back. His brother was so wise for his age. Tyler wished he had spoken to him before about all of his concerns. Somehow, clarity was sinking in. He needed to work on his relationship with God. He needed to read His Bible more and make wiser choices. He wanted to be better- better for his family, better for Emily, and better for God. He looked at the time on the radio display.

01:18. He had a few hours left to catch up on some sleep before his test that morning.

The traffic light flashed green.

Noah angled himself to face the road again and entered the intersection.

Tyler spoke at the same time. "Listen, Noah, I'm-"

A blinding light came from nowhere, followed by a devastating crashing sound that ripped through the entire vehicle. Tyler felt as if he had been lifted into the air and was plummeting down. The sounds of tires screeched around him, and suddenly, thick darkness enveloped him like a rogue wave.

Tyler lurched upright in bed, his mouth agape in a silent scream. His eyes squinted through the unfamiliar darkness, and his heart rate quickened. He looked around rapidly, the realization slowly dawning on him that he was in Noah's room and had been dreaming. He let out a deep breath and held his chest.

Beads of sweat ran down his forehead, and he wiped at it with the back of his hand, swinging his legs over the bed and sitting upright. His T-shirt was damp. He pulled it over his head and threw it on the floor. He felt his hands tremble. Every memory from that night tore him apart.

He reached for his phone on the bedside table and unlocked it to check the time. His heart dropped. *Not again*, he thought.

01:18.

He stared at the digits. This had to be some kind of joke, although he didn't find it funny. He threw the phone on the bed and sighed deeply. The dream of those moments with Noah was so real. He could almost feel the support of his brother's arms around him and hear his words again. Tyler felt his eyes well up. He leaned back in the bed and stared at the ceiling, the back of his hand across his forehead.

It was all his fault. If he hadn't fallen into temptation that night, things would have been different. If he hadn't acted like a fool, Noah would still be alive, probably married with children of his own to pass his wisdom and teachings down to. If the urge to fit into the world hadn't overcome him, Emily would still be his. Tyler squeezed his eyes shut to block it all out, wondering if things could ever be new again.

"Come now, and let us reason together…"

Tyler jolted up from the bed once more. He knew the voice was real this time. He was not imagining things. He quickly got off the bed and walked towards the bedroom door. The voice had to be his father on the phone with someone. Tyler opened the door slightly and tried to listen. There was silence. He let out a sigh and closed the door, leaning his back against it.

Returning home had brought up so many emotions within him that he had probably started creating voices in his subconscious. Either that, or his guilt was consuming him, making him go crazy.

Noah's words from that night rang in his ears again. *When there is a great purpose on your life, the enemy will try and look for an opening to come in and destroy you.*

Tyler felt a stabbing pain in his gut as he thought about those words. People always blamed the enemy when things went wrong. But, what if the enemy wasn't always to blame? Tyler had to live with the hard reality that his brother's life and purpose had been cut short because of his own actions; his own disobedience.

And no matter how many years had passed, Tyler's heart could not find rest after knowing that.

Nine

The coffee shop drew the most traffic in the mornings. Customers were always grabbing their cappuccinos to go or stopping by for a quick breakfast before their daily activities began.

Emily found her spot towards the back of the café, where she had a clear view of everything. She enjoyed being at her coffee shop. It gave her the chance to meet and greet people in the neighborhood, and it also reminded her of God's goodness in her life. It had always been her dream to own a cosy eatery where people could read, attend to projects, have meetings, and enjoy the warmth of one another's company.

She opened her laptop and began scrolling through some of her unread emails. One email was from her mother, suggesting honeymoon destinations with beautiful images and informative links to click on. Emily smiled while shaking her head, and typed a quick reply.

Thanks Mom! Will have a look later. She hit send.

Her neck ached, so she kneaded her fingers around the base of it. She hadn't slept well the night before, either. Every time she closed her eyes, she would see Tyler's face again.

Before leaving on business, Ian had asked her if there was anything he needed to worry about, seeing as Tyler was now back. Emily had told him the truth.

The answer was no.

She and Tyler had history and many unresolved discussions, but that didn't mean Ian had to worry. Emily meant that.

She went over one of the emails from her caterer, confirming the number of wedding guests who were vegetarians. The wedding date was drawing closer. Emily expected to feel more excited going through wedding emails, but the events of the last day weighed heavily on her.

She did want to marry Ian. A lifetime ago, the man's face whom she believed would be waiting for her at the front of any aisle was Tyler's, but life didn't always turn out the way a person hoped. Emily believed that, maybe, it was a good thing. God always knew better, right? The little girl dreams she once had all came to an abrupt halt many years ago, and that could have been for her good. After all, one of her favorite Bible verses said that all things work out well for those who love the Lord. She did love the Lord, so she had to believe her life was unraveling the way Heaven had planned it.

Besides, Emily wasn't going to risk her plans with Ian all because Tyler Hill had returned like a whirlwind, leaving her scrambling through the debris of their past.

Candice walked towards her and placed a cappuccino with cream on the table. "Have you heard from him as yet?" she asked Emily curiously.

Emily pulled the cappuccino closer and swiped the cream off with her spoon, replying, "No, he's been in meetings since this morning."

Candice smiled. "I wasn't talking about Ian." She gave Emily a pointed look as she lowered her voice. "I meant Tyler."

"No, I haven't heard from him." Emily's answer was quick, but polite. "Why would I? I doubt he has anything to say for himself after all these years." She continued typing a response to the caterer and broke eye contact with Candice.

Emily wasn't expecting Tyler to reach out to her now that he had returned, but she was hoping to see him before he left town again. Perhaps speaking to him before her marriage would do her some good in getting answers to years of unanswered questions. Nothing in life was more uncomfortable than unfinished business.

Candice seemed to have received the message that the Tyler-topic was closed for discussion. She touched Emily's arm. "Take it easy, Em. We can grab lunch later if you're keen and chat then."

Emily looked up at her and smiled, grateful for a friend like her. "Yes, I'd like that a lot."

A group of teenagers from the church walked into the coffee shop. They were part of the youth group and often frequented the café before or after school. Candice had disappeared in the back, so Emily stood up and headed over towards the group.

"Good morning, guys! What's the orders today?"

The blonde girl was Paula. She checked the menu quickly. "Em, I'll just take a coffee to go," she said while flipping her hair back. "We have a pop quiz in an hour. I'm going to need all the caffeine I can get."

"I'll take a peach iced tea, please." Claire opened her textbook and started whisking through the pages frantically while saying, "I am so stressed about this test Emily. I just know I am going to fail this." Her tone was dramatic, and the other teens laughed at her.

Emily smiled at Claire. "How about you refresh my memory on what we learned last week at the youth meeting?"

Claire rolled her eyes playfully, groaning, "Emily, I can barely remember what I did last night." She passed her friends a look to help her out.

Luke spoke next. Emily had a soft spot for him. He was a foster child with a rough upbringing behind him. After joining the youth group, his confidence spiked.

"Emily taught us that the Bible says the power of life and death lies in our tongue and with our words," he explained. "So, it's important to choose our words carefully."

The others gave Luke a high-five, and a playful round of applause resounded around the group.

Emily smiled at them, saying, "Exactly. So, Claire, do you want to try that again?"

Claire cocked her head to the side and let out a deep sigh, closing her book. "I'll take a peach iced tea, please." She smiled at them all; her voice a little bit more upbeat than before. "Because, I have to get to school to ace this test!"

The others chuckled, and Emily nodded in agreement. "Your orders are coming right up!" She made her way to the front desk and punched in the orders on the screen.

Candice joined her, wiping her hands on her apron while saying, "Here, let me do it. You get back to your emails."

Emily thanked her and made her way back to her spot, refreshing her mail. She was just about to draft a new one when her phone buzzed on the table. She picked it up and read the text message from Ian.

I miss you already.

Emily found herself smiling at the screen as she typed back. *Then get back to your meetings so you can come home.* She hit send and instantly saw that he had read it and was typing his response.

Ian's profile picture caught her eye, and she opened it to view it. It was a photo from the night he had proposed to her. He had changed his display image between the day before and that morning. Emily didn't want to read too deeply into his reasons why. Maybe, it was his way of subtly reminding her that all was well between them. She zoomed in and looked at the photo.

In the picture, she was smiling while holding either side of Ian's face with her hands, the diamond ring on her finger sparkling in the glare of the photo flash. Ian was grinning ear to ear.

Something curled in her stomach. It had been a pivotal moment for her. When she had first met Ian, she was determined to avoid any romantic entanglement with him. She knew that he was the whole package, and getting involved with him meant saying goodbye to the possibility of her and Tyler ever again. When Ian had proposed a year ago, Emily knew what saying yes meant. It meant that she had to let go of the past, and forge ahead with a new future.

She was still staring at the photo when a figure walked up to her table and paused momentarily before speaking. "Hi…"

Emily glanced up from the phone, and her breath caught in her throat. She hadn't seen him approaching. How had he found her café?

He had a nervous look on his face, but flashed her a courteous smile while he touched the chair opposite her. "Am I disturbing you?"

Emily put her phone face down while sucking in a breath. "Hi…" She paused and motioned at the empty seat opposite her saying, "No, you can sit."

Tyler pulled the chair back and sat down slowly. He was wearing jeans and a white T-shirt. A combination he always looked so good in. It emphasized his chocolate brown eyes. Emily studied him. It felt surreal seeing him right in front of her again. She almost wanted to reach out and touch him.

He slid her a familiar set of keys across the table. "My mother said you needed to have these before the evening."

Emily looked at the keys. So, that's how he had found her. She wondered whether he had come to the café just to save his mother the trip or if the keys were an excuse to see her. She wouldn't dare ask him. She took the keys and dropped them into her bag on the floor.

"Thank you. Ian has the other set, and he's out of town on business," she said while tucking a strand of hair behind her ear. "I have a youth meeting tonight." She swallowed the knot in her throat and observed him. If he was uncomfortable being there with her, he didn't show it. He appeared much more relaxed than he had been the day before.

Candice came up to the table, a menu in her hand, but her eyes curiously darting between Emily and Tyler's. "Morning, can I get you something?"

Emily watched Tyler quickly glance at the menu, and he returned Candice's smile, replying, "Sure, can I just grab a coffee? Nothing to eat, though, thanks."

Candice jotted it down quickly, and Emily motioned with her hand between them to do the necessary introductions. "Candice, this is Tyler. Pastor Mike and Beth's son." She looked at Tyler and continued, "Tyler, this is Candice. She's a good friend of mine and the manager of the café."

For a brief moment, Emily felt lousy for not introducing Tyler as a friend or even as an old friend of hers. But her introduction had already slipped out of her mouth, and it was too late to take it back and rephrase it. Besides, the term *friend* was a little bit tricky at this stage. And Candice knew all about Tyler Hill already.

Tyler extended his hand to shake Candice's. "It's nice to meet you, Candice." He smiled in a teasing manner, and Emily felt her heart skip a beat at the sight. It took her right back to nineteen whenever he would playfully mock her.

She pushed the memories aside as he spoke to Candice, asking her, "So is Emmy a good boss to work for? She was quite pushy from what I remember."

Candice grinned and looked at Emily cheekily. "Then, she hasn't changed much. I'll get your coffee and leave you two alone."

As she walked off, she turned to look at Emily and mouthed something which Emily made out as the words *'he's gorgeous'*. Emily ignored her and looked back at Tyler, who was admiring the café. He *was* gorgeous, no doubt. But, beneath his attractive features remained a lost and broken man.

His eyes found hers as he spoke. "You always wanted to do this, Emmy. And you actually did it. It's really amazing."

Emily tried to ignore how he made her feel whenever he called her that. She kept her tone pleasant. "I'm glad you got a chance to see it. But, you can't truly appreciate it until you've tasted the pancakes. They've been on quite the journey to get here. I think you would be very proud."

He laughed out loud at her comment, and Emily found herself grinning. The sound of his laughter stirred an unexpected longing within her. She wondered if he felt the same in her presence.

Probably not, she thought.

After all, he had broken it off with her. He wouldn't have done that had he still cared for her.

Candice brought the coffee to the table, and Tyler thanked her while reaching for a sachet of sugar before asking, "So, what's this youth meeting you have to go to tonight? Aren't we past the age of youths?"

The light-hearted mood hadn't changed between them, despite the years that had. Emily felt herself ease back into old patterns of enjoying the banter with him. "Speak for yourself," she chuckled. "The last twelve years haven't been your best friend." She was messing with him, and his grin told her that he took it in good stride. He had never looked better, but she couldn't say that to him without crossing dangerous territory.

"Well, the years have been good to you, Emmy. You still look the same."

His comment caused a heat to fill her cheeks. The atmosphere between them changed, and Emily felt that suffocating sensation creep up her neck. The way he looked at her made it impossible for her to guard her emotions. The way he said her name awoke butterflies in her that had been dormant for so many years.

His eyes fell to her hand, and Emily knew that the ring on her finger disturbed the moment. She moved her hand under the table without even realizing why she did it.

He put his fist to his mouth, clearing his throat and sitting upright. He took a sip of his coffee and leaned back, asking, "So, my Dad mentioned that you run the youth program on your own." His expression grew softer, but the playfulness in his tone had dissipated. "The one in honor of Noah?"

Emily felt a lump in her throat at the sound of Noah's name from his mouth. They had never spoken about Noah since the accident, and she felt as if she was in unchartered waters. She also wondered what else he and Pastor Mike had shared concerning her. As she tucked another strand of hair behind her ear, she saw something flicker in his eyes. She tried to ignore it, but knew what he was thinking.

Twelve years may have passed, but they remembered the details.

She kept her tone natural. "Yeah, I've been running it for about four years now. It's for the teenagers." She pointed towards the group of teens who had come in earlier. Tyler followed her direction and looked over his shoulder at the youngsters as she continued explaining.

"Those are some of them. God is doing some great things in their lives." She took a breath. "The blonde girl, Paula, used to suffer with depression until she started joining. The smaller guy is Luke. He had a rough childhood but is one of the sweetest boys you will ever meet. Claire never went a weekend without partying, and now she's an A-student and president of a Christian club in school."

Emily saw the astonishment on Tyler's face as she rattled off the change in each teenager. She decided to continue boldly while she had his attention. "It is a much-needed program for this season in their lives." She heard the nervousness in her own voice as she continued, saying, "A person's teenage years can really shape their future."

He looked up at her from his coffee, his expression suddenly rigid. She knew that her words had touched a sensitive spot, raising his walls again. She watched his eyes grow weary, and she silently scolded herself for going there so soon. He framed the coffee cup with his hand and his lips pinched together.

Emily tried to keep the conversation from falling flat. She didn't want him to get up and leave yet. "You should come by tonight and see what's been going on for yourself." The suggestion had fallen out of her mouth before she had thought it through. Once again, she was uncertain if she had made the situation even worse. Pushing him towards the things of God and faith never did much good in the past.

A strange shadow flashed around his eyes. He held her gaze, and she couldn't make out what he was thinking. He checked his watch and flashed her a gracious smile while saying, "I've got to go. My mother wants me to help her at my grandad's place with some boxes."

He took out his wallet, and Emily interjected, lifting her palm from the table. "Don't worry about it," she said while smiling. "It's on the house."

She noticed that he hadn't even finished his coffee. It was probably her fault. He had just been warming up, and she had to say something that put him on edge. He returned the smile and pushed his chair back to leave.

"Thanks, Emmy. I guess I'll see you around?"

Emily felt the unexpected sting of tears make its way around her eyes. She didn't know what was wrong with her. The last time he had said goodbye to her, it had been for twelve years. Now, she feared that any goodbye could be the last time she would see him again. She still had so much she wanted to ask and say. Before she could filter her question, it tumbled out of her mouth, catching him off guard.

"When?" She felt humiliated at her desperate tone, and quickly rephrased it. "I mean, how long are you really staying for?"

The atmosphere between them became charged. He looked at her in a way that he used to- as if she was the only girl in the room. Emily held her breath, waiting for his answer. The chemistry between them was undeniable.

He shrugged, his eyes never leaving hers, saying, "I don't know yet, Emmy."

Her face must have reflected despair. His eyes earnestly studied hers. It was as if he were about to say something but chose to bite his tongue. He finally spoke, saying, "I will say goodbye, though. Before I leave."

The silence between them was almost deafening. Emily fought the urge to get up and go to him. She clasped her hands together and felt her engagement ring brush her skin. Before she could say anything, he broke his gaze from hers and walked off. Emily watched him drop some cash in the tip-jar as he made his way out the front door.

She let out a heavy sigh. She had tried so hard to maintain a façade, but Tyler was always able to see through the surface of who she was- right down to where she harbored the pain. If he had stayed even a moment longer, Emily didn't know what could have been said or done.

Candice made her way to Emily cautiously. "Is everything okay?" she asked. "That was some serious tension between you two."

Emily nodded slowly. "Yeah, twelve years worth."

Candice must have sensed Emily's disposition, so she tried to clear the air humorously, by asking, "Is it too soon for me to get his number then?"

Emily let out a single laugh when all she really wanted to do was cry. "I don't even have his number, Candice!" She let out a sad sigh and picked up her cellphone from the table, noticing the unread text message from Ian. It had come through moments before Tyler had appeared. She opened it to read Ian's response to her earlier message.

Spoken like a true wife-to-be. Love you. He had added a heart icon at the end of his message.

Emily looked up at Candice, feeling conflicted. Candice must have understood her plight. She took the seat opposite her and patted Emily's hand. "Em, maybe Tyler coming back home is God's way of giving you what you've been waiting for all these years."

"And what's that?" Emily asked.

"Closure," she said while squeezing Emily's hand. "Closure, and a chance to say goodbye properly."

Her words were not what Emily was expecting. But then again, Emily couldn't blame her for thinking that was the answer. After all, Emily kept telling everyone there was nothing to worry about now that Tyler was back. She had kept harping on how she just wanted closure.

She bit her lip. Was that really all she wanted?

A customer tapped the bell at the front desk, and Candice hurriedly made her way there.

Emily pondered Candice's words. There were many things she had been waiting for and wanting from Tyler after all these years.

But saying goodbye to him was never it.

The chapter in their lives had once ended so abruptly that all Emily really wanted was to have had the chance to see what the story could have been.

Tyler's grip tightened on the steering wheel of the car even as he stared at the name above the café.

Emmy's.

That spoke volumes. He gritted his teeth and leaned his head back against the seat. He knew to see her wasn't going to be easy, but he didn't expect the feelings that had come knocking at his heart's door once again. Over the years, he had grown accustomed to flirting with women and being in control of every situation, never letting his guard down and never revealing any genuine emotions. His connection with women was nothing more than the physical.

But Emily was not just any other woman. She was the one. She had always been the one. He had known that since being fifteen. Emily had a way about her that made him feel at ease and like he belonged somewhere. Nobody looked at him the way she did. And when her green eyes met him, every wall he had built came crashing down.

He watched the group of youngsters leave the café; the ones Emily had mentioned were a part of the church's youth group. They looked a lot like he had years ago; carefree and filled with dreams and purpose.

Emily was right. A person's teenage years really did shape them for the future. Because there he was, alone in a car, looking longingly at a woman inside a café who he knew was a lifetime away from him. All because of a foolish decision he had made as a teenager.

Tyler sighed as he watched her work on her laptop through the glass windows.

I never meant to hurt you, Emmy, he thought.

If she could peer into the windows of his heart, she would see that. She had just been collateral damage in the war he was waging with himself.

Everything in him had yearned to reach across that table, take her in his arms, and never let her go. But that would have been reckless. And since he had learned the hard way about being reckless once before, he wasn't about to make that mistake again and possibly destroy a life she was moving ahead with.

Amid the familiar banter and the electric pull between them, the diamond ring on her finger had pummeled him back to reality.

Not only did that diamond stone reflect the brilliance of the light that bounced off of it, but it also revealed all he had destroyed and let slip through his fingers years ago.

Ten

The house held a forlorn emptiness. It no longer had the inviting warmth that Beth had grown accustomed to over the years. Losing Bill was one thing, but not seeing him pace the hallways or chuckle whilst cooking dinner made her heart ache.

She continued packing some of the items into boxes and leaving it aside for the church. Bill had been in the process of giving away some of his winter gear to the less privileged, but he had not finished doing it before he became unwell and passed on. Beth's eyes welled up with tears as she looked around the room. It would take a while before she could start packing Bill's personal belongings away.

It had taken her years before she could even move Noah's things into storage.

She checked her watch and knew Tyler would be arriving shortly to help her. She had sent him on an errand to deliver the church keys at Emily's café, and Beth wondered if they both had decided to catch up. It was something they needed to do, whether they believed it or not. Beth respected Emily's engagement to Ian. Still, Beth was a firm believer that people needed to be entirely sure about where their hearts stood before making huge decisions- such as marriage, or even leaving town for that matter. Making hasty decisions based on current emotions never ended well for anyone.

Beth stood up from the floor whilst dusting her hands on her caramel-colored skirt. She made her way down the hallway to the kitchen. Large bouquets lined the kitchen counters, all from friends and family who had come to the funeral. The sight of the flowers resonated a familiar sting within her. She remembered the bountiful deliveries when Noah had passed away. Back then, there were double the number of bouquets being delivered all over the place- to the hospital, to the church, to the grave, and to their home. Some flowers were to pass on condolences for the loss of Noah, and others were a get well soon gesture for Tyler. Flowers spoke a language that not many could do at a time of deep sorrow and tragic loss.

Beth opened the kitchen windows to let the fresh air in and found herself staring at the garden outside. The house was beautiful, the garden enormous and manicured. She could easily picture Noah and Tyler playing outside, climbing trees and getting mud on their shoes. They always preferred being at their grandfather's house than their own home.

Beth wondered when Michael planned on having the talk with Tyler about the contents of the letter that Bill had left behind for him. It wasn't her place to say anything about the house, so she wasn't planning to. But the thought of the inevitable discussion gave her anxiety.

A picture on the kitchen wall made her smile. It was one taken about twenty years ago at a thanksgiving dinner with the entire family. *We were all so happy and whole back then,* she thought.

She allowed her mind to travel back to the devastating memory of that night. She remembered it distinctly. The clock had struck past two-thirty that morning when Michael had received the call. As ministers of a large number of congregants, a call at that hour usually came for several reasons. Mostly unpleasant ones. Beth remembered tossing over in bed, wondering who could be sick or in need of help at that time of night. The thought even crossed her mind that it could have been Bill. She just never expected the horror of what was to come.

She knew Tyler and Emily had been out at a party, but believed they had returned. They had never stayed out past their curfew before. Noah had been at a meeting planning an outreach trip and he had come home early. She and Michael had dinner with him before he went off to bed.

Beth remembered the moment when Michael answered the phone. Someone spoke on the other end, and within a few seconds, Michael sat up frantically in the bed. His voice was louder and distressed, asking, "Are they okay?"

His eyes darted to Beth as he flung the covers off of him and put the sidelight on, while searching for his clothes. Beth sat up, every bit of sleep dissolving. She knew by that one look on her husband's face that something awful had happened.

They were told very few details on the phone- Noah and Tyler were involved in a terrible accident, and they were to come to the hospital as quickly as possible. Beth had been so confused, wondering if there had been a mistake. But before leaving the house, she had noticed that both her sons were not asleep in their rooms as she had hoped.

It confirmed the possibility of the nightmare they were about to face.

The entire drive to the hospital was in slow motion. Beth couldn't breathe or think straight. Michael's grip on the steering wheel revealed his whitened knuckles. He didn't say a word to her the whole drive there. He was just praying under his breath. Beth was frantic, wondering if Emily or any other youngster was in the car with them. She kept telling herself that God would not let anything bad happen and that all would be well. God's protection was on their family. Wasn't it?

When they had arrived at the hospital, their entire world imploded. Beth had noticed two police officers standing near the vending machine, speaking in hushed tones. She convinced herself that they were not there for Michael or her.

A doctor whom they had known for many years pulled them aside into a waiting room. As he made space for them to walk in front of him, he had turned to the two officers, nodding slowly. Beth still recalled how those two acts alone had given her anxiety. It was never a good sign when people had to be ushered into a quiet room in a hospital to receive information. If all was well, the doctor could have spoken to them anywhere. Also, it bothered her that the two officers were standing nearby, almost waiting for the doctor to be done speaking with them.

Beth had a firm grip on Michael's arm as the doctor explained that the boys were driving home when a truck had run a red light at an intersection and had hit Tyler's vehicle at an alarming speed on the driver's side. As a result of the accident, Tyler sustained head injuries, broken bones, and was unresponsive at the scene. When the doctor mentioned he was in ICU in a coma, Beth felt the floor give way. The information rocked her to her core.

The doctor's words and medical terms were sounding muffled to her ears. He was speaking about trauma, scans, tests, and brain activity, all of which Beth couldn't understand. She wasn't a medical professional to know what it all meant, but she knew it was not good. A coma was never good. The doctor had mentioned something about Tyler being intoxicated too. Beth couldn't understand that part. Tyler had been at a party with Emily, but she knew her sons didn't drink alcohol.

Michael asked the next question, his words a frightened whisper. "What about Noah? How is he?"

Beth would never forget the look on the doctor's face for as long as she lived. His eyes darted to the two police officers, and then quickly found hers. The words struggled to come out of his mouth. He had let out a deep breath, and his eyes were dark with sorrow as he shook his head and said, "I am sorry…"

Those were three words she would never forget. Beth did not remember much else that followed after that moment. The doctor had continued talking about the impact, the injuries, and it being too late for Noah by the time the paramedics had arrived. The words were drowning out from the echo of her shrill screams through the waiting room. She had fallen to the ground in a pitiful ball. Michael had let out a gut-wrenching cry, one she had never heard before. His arms were around her, repeating the words, "*No, Lord*" over and over and over again.

They wept on the hospital floor for what felt like an eternity.

In one moment, their son's life was gone. It was surreal how many flashbacks and memories came flooding into her mind as she stayed in a crumpled pile on the cold hospital tiles. The same hospital that had brought them news of both her sons' arrival was now a place of mourning for the loss of one of them.

Beth remembered the first moment when the nurses had placed Noah on her chest. His baby fingers had curled around her thumb, and she didn't know if she could ever love anything more. She remembered the first time he had fallen off his bicycle, knees bleeding from not wearing his gear but smiling bravely as she cleaned the wounds. She recalled every goodnight kiss before bed and every good morning hug before school. She remembered his doting behavior when Tyler was born, not allowing anyone to carry his baby brother without first washing their hands. She thought of all his hopes and dreams to be used by God for the souls of the lost.

And in a single moment, he was gone.

Beth couldn't even remember what her last words were to him before he went off to bed that night. Had she told him that she loved him? Had she told him how proud she was of the man he was becoming?

Even amidst their grief over Noah, another looming fear took hold of them; the fear of possibly losing Tyler too. The doctors provided as much medical information as they could, but always ended the conversation in a way that rarely provided them much hope. If Tyler came out of the coma, his real condition would still require assessment. Those situations were a case by case basis, and nothing was for sure. Noah had lost his life, and Tyler was fighting for his.

It was a parent's worse nightmare.

"Mom?" Tyler's voice broke Beth out of the memory, and she realized that she had been holding her breath, crying in the kitchen. She quickly wiped at her tears and inhaled. The sight of her youngest son in the kitchen just made her heart leap, reminding her that this part was real- he was healthy and alive. He was a miracle.

If only he realized that.

She flashed Tyler a smile as she found her voice. "Hi, Dear…"

He had most likely come in moments ago while she was deep in thought. His face looked despondent. Being at his grandfather's house was bound to bring back tons of memories for him. Coming back was just as hard on him as it was for everyone, even though he didn't show his emotions as openly as they all did.

Tyler slowly walked towards her, and put his arms around her. He was much taller than she, so she pressed her cheek against his chest, squeezing him to her. Much like she use to do when he had been a child, afraid of the dark or when the bullies in his school had upset him. He had always been different from Noah. He was more unsure of himself. And lost.

He pulled back and gave her a comforting smile, saying, "It's strange being here without him."

Beth looked at him blankly, uncertain who he was referring to. The truth was that it was strange being there without both Noah and Bill. She assumed he was referring to his grandfather because he never spoke about Noah after the accident. Tyler circled the kitchen area slowly, fingering the flowers on the counter before shoving his hands in his pocket.

"He kept everything the same as I last remembered it." He leaned against the counter. "Were you thinking of him, just now when I walked in?"

Beth sniffed and let out a sigh. "I was thinking about everything," she said. "Sadly, he's not here anymore, but it's wonderful to see you back in this house. It has felt empty without you around." She smiled. "Even your grandad felt it."

Tyler remained quiet as he searched her face. If he wanted to say something, he had stopped himself.

Beth soldiered on while the opportunity was rife. "It must feel strange being back. Do you miss home at all?" she asked.

A silence hung in the air. The only sound Beth could hear was the faint running of the stream in the backyard.

Tyler worried his lower lip before replying. "I don't know how to answer that, Mom, without sounding like a horrible son. I have mixed feelings about everything. It's so hard to explain."

Beth tried not to look as hurt as she felt by his response. She could see the honesty and struggle written on his face. It brought a tightening in her throat.

She sighed while saying, "Well, that sort of answers the question." She crossed her arms and looked around. "I guess all a mother and father want for their child is for them to be happy and at peace." She found his eyes again. "So, are you?" She cocked her head to the side, waiting for his answer. When he didn't answer, she probed again. "Are you happy and at peace, Tyler?"

A defeated look fell across his face as he rubbed his forehead. "I don't know, Mom. I don't think so. What is happiness and peace suppose to look like after all that we have been through?"

Beth felt for her son. He was so lost and dejected, but yet still so proud to change. She walked towards him and took her place next to him, studying his defeated posture. "Son, you cannot keep living your life not knowing the answer to those questions." She saw the emotion in his eyes and wondered whether something had transpired between him and Emily. She kept her voice light when she asked, "Was Emily at the café when you dropped the keys off?"

"Yeah, she was. We chatted a bit," he said as he looked down. "It felt strange speaking to her after all this time. She has her own business, she's engaged, and she's running the youth at church." He paused and let his arms drop to his sides. "It's weird how places have remained the same after all these years. But the people and their lives have changed so much."

Beth let out a little chuckle and touched her son's face tenderly. "That's what happens when you let all this confusion-" she poked at his temple with her finger before continuing, "steal away precious time. You miss out on a lot in the lives of the people you love." She paused. "And who love you."

Tyler let his eyes fall to the ground.

Beth knew she had made her point.

Everything about his grandad's house brought him right back to his childhood. Standing in the driveway and looking around made Tyler feel as if everything had frozen from that day, years ago. As if he had never left. His eyes darted from the white fence, to the porch, to the bird feeder. A sigh escaped his lips at the sight of it all. *I would do anything to go back to that day*, he thought.

Countless alternative scenarios played in his mind from that day. He could have taken Emily to that movie and dinner, and been back home in bed before midnight. He could have helped his brother on the outreach itinerary as promised, both safe at home with their parents. He could have gone to the party, and followed his gut to leave the moment the warning had come.

Tyler shook his head slowly at the thoughts of it all. It was no use thinking about all of it now.

He leaned against the car and waited for his mother to bring out the last box from inside. He gazed around the property, recalling the desire he once had to own the house one day. It was the home he had hoped would be his and Emily's. It was all planned out- a story uninterrupted and perfect until it wasn't anymore.

His mother's words about confusion stealing away precious time rang in his mind. He often questioned himself in the same way that she had. Was he happy? Was he at peace? How could he find a sense of normalcy after everything that had happened? Without warning, a scribble of words appeared in his mind.

Happy are the people whose God is the Lord.

Tyler felt his throat constrict. This sort of thing was happening to him quite often since he had come back. Tyler pondered the words. Was it true? Was he unhappy and without peace, because he had walked away from God? An unexpected breeze surrounded him, and Tyler felt the hairs on his arms rise. He shook it off, convincing himself that he was just growing overly-sensitive and emotional.

Seeing Emily in the morning had evoked certain sentiments within him. And shortly after seeing her, he was at his grandfather's home, questioning whether he was happy or not. The whirlwind of emotions were coming and going in waves, pulling him further out into the sea of despair.

His plan had been to attend the funeral and then leave. Not to immerse himself in yesterday's seasons. Tyler knew that he could have gone back to his regular life by now. But something was holding him back from leaving just yet.

He just didn't know what it was.

His mother walked down the porch steps carrying the last box. He met her halfway retrieving it from her hands. She locked the front door before making her way towards him, asking, "Will you drop those boxes off at the church tonight? It will be open for the youth meeting."

Tyler wondered whether his mother was doing that sort of thing intentionally, but he didn't argue or fight her on it. Emily had invited him to the youth meeting to see what it was all about. He hadn't answered Emily out of fear that he would upset her if he said that visiting the meeting didn't interest him. The further he could be from the church, the better. But he also couldn't push aside the urge within him to see her face again. Seeing her again had made him realize how much he had missed her in his life.

And, there was still so much he wanted to say to her.

He shielded his eyes from the sun as he looked up at the house. It was odd not seeing his grandfather stand in the doorway to wave goodbye as they pulled away, or to see him sitting on the rocking chair on the front porch with his famous lemonade and newspaper in hand.

Something his grandfather had said to him on that day echoed in his heart. *God always a special blessing for the youngest one.* Tyler gritted his teeth. Even if that was true, he believed he had forfeited his right to any special blessing twelve years ago.

His mother came to his side, also looking in his direction, saying, "It's a beautiful home, isn't it?"

Tyler couldn't agree with her more. He planted his hands on his hips, asking, "What does Dad plan on doing with it?"

His question was sincere. Tyler couldn't imagine the house belonging to anyone else, other than his grandad. He could remember his grandfather's words on the day of the accident. He had said that it was his dream to have generations of their family live and love in that house. Noah was no longer alive to fulfill that wish, although it had never been one of Noah's desires. It had always been Tyler's.

But Tyler knew that he couldn't fulfill it either.

Fulfilling that promise would mean returning to that which he was trying to get far away from. His mother was quiet for a moment before she walked to the passenger side of the car and got in.

That's strange, Tyler thought.

His mother hadn't answered his question.

of faith, grounded in love and kindness. What was God's plan in taking Noah, and leaving Tyler behind, fighting for his life?

The doctors continuously spoke about tests and about monitoring him. They said that the family was to hope for the best and to pray for a miracle. Emily knew one thing for sure; nothing would change how she felt about Tyler even if he woke up a different person. She would be at his side no matter what the circumstances were.

Emily blamed herself for a lot of what had happened that night. She had phoned Noah, awaking him from his sleep and begging him to drag Tyler out from Ricky's house because of his foolishness. If she hadn't done that, things could have been different. Even if she had called Noah five minutes later than she had, he would have been five minutes delayed in getting to Tyler, and he would have made it through that green light, avoiding the collision of the truck altogether. So many scenarios similar to that one played in her head that it made her dizzy.

What was even more difficult to bear, was relaying the events of that night to Beth and Pastor Mike. Emily was the only one who could provide answers of why Noah and Tyler were driving back home together. And why Tyler was intoxicated. It was best coming from her before they were to hear different versions of the story from others in the church and neighborhood. People were already starting to gossip and spread false rumors about the events of that night. Some were saying that Tyler had driven whilst drunk. Others were saying that both the pastors' sons were secret party animals

Emily pulled Tyler's bandaged hand closer to her lips and pressed her mouth to his skin. His words to her, before they had entered the party, had found a special place in her heart. He had told her that despite his struggles, she was the only thing he was truly sure about. Emily felt tears trickle down her face. She could taste the saltiness of them as she whispered a prayer, *"Lord, save him, please. Don't take him away. Don't be done with him just yet. Give us a miracle."*

She opened her eyes and waited for some sign or miracle as she had asked for. She hoped that some voice would enter the room and reassure her that all was going to be well. She wondered if Tyler would feel her beside him and if he would move or open his eyes. She searched his scarred face, waiting for him to turn over and flash her that lovable smile she had fallen for. But nothing happened.

Pastor Mike entered the room, a coffee in his hand. His hair was disheveled, and his shirt had multiple creases as if he had been sleeping in it. He held out the coffee to her.

Emily reached for it, her eyes desperate as she asked, "Any news from the doctor?"

Pastor Mike rounded the bed to the other side and touched his son's head, his voice thick with emotion. "They are running more tests and watching his vitals closely for signs of improvement." His eyes were sunken. He spoke through gritted teeth. "Even if he does wake up, we don't know what sort of situation we are looking at. They will have to test for responsiveness and start the road for therapy and recovery based on his condition."

With each word, Emily's heart sank deeper into her stomach. She fought back tears, unable to believe that they were talking about Tyler in such a manner. He was the healthiest and most active young man she knew. It had been a week straight from hell. Everything was a blur as if the days were just blending into one long abyss.

She sipped the coffee and kept her voice low, just in case Tyler could hear her. "How is Beth doing? My mom tried calling her last night."

Pastor Mike pinched the bridge of his nose as he replied, "She's not doing good, Em. She is going to take the evening shift, so I told her to try and rest now."

Emily felt an ache within her. She put the coffee on the ground and found Tyler's hand again. She let out a sad-sounding sighed. "I've been sitting here thinking about a message you once preached about looking for the glass-half-full in every situation. Because that's what helps you stay grateful in all things…"

Pastor Mike kept his head down, and his eyes were weary.

Emily let out a choked cry. "I can't see what good is in this whole situation, Pastor Mike." She wiped at her tears, angrily. Pastor Mike left his spot and made his way towards her, bending down and wrapping her in his arms like she was a little girl.

Emily sobbed into his chest, and her words were all muffled against him, her tears wetting his shirt. "It's been days, and he hasn't even flinched. What good can we find in this situation?" She wiped at her runny nose and searched Pastor Mike's eyes.

Tears welled up in his own eyes as he pulled back from her.

He moved towards Tyler and put his hand over his son's hand. His eyes found hers again. "The good in this situation is that he's still here." He paused, and Emily saw him swallow back the emotion. He looked at her earnestly, continuing, "The doctor said we were lucky that he was even pulled out of that wreck alive, breathing on his own. The papers called him the miracle survivor." He took a breath. "I don't believe in luck, Em. I believe it's part of a purpose that he is even here right now, fighting to wake up."

Emily couldn't help but marvel at the man. Even now, at this time, he managed to find something he could share with her to comfort her, even though he was struggling himself.

The accident had been horrific. Tyler's car had become nothing but a chunk of twisted metal. The impact killed Noah instantly. People who had heard about or seen the images from the accident knew that it was a miracle that Tyler was even removed from the wreck, still alive and in one piece. The doctors said that there was still a chance that he would wake up and live a normal life because they had seen worse cases turn out well.

Emily reached towards Tyler's cut and bruised face, and brushed the corner of his hair near his ear. "I am praying so much for the moment he wakes up, Pastor Mike. That's all I want."

Pastor Mike ran his hand down the length of his son's arm before finding Emily's eyes, saying, "Pray for another thing, Em."

Emily waited for his request.

When he spoke, his voice dripped with a heaviness. Almost like he foresaw something that she couldn't. "Pray for his days after that," he said with deep emotion. He paused before continuing. "Something tells me that if Tyler comes out of this, he's going to face an even greater battle with himself."

It was at that moment that Emily suddenly realized the horrifying truth. Even if Tyler woke up, they still had to face another devastating moment- the moment when they told him that the brother who had tried to get him home safely had not made it out of the accident alive.

Pastor Mike was right; the battle was far from over.

Tyler was overwhelmed with a thickness all around him. His body felt as if someone had dressed him in woolen clothing and had thrown him into deep waters. It was as if a force was pulling him downwards into a never-ending hole. There was an occasional whirring and beeping around him. Muffled voices filtered through the darkness and he couldn't open his eyes no matter how hard he tried. He didn't know where he was or why his body felt so strange- as if it was not his.

A flashback came to him about drinking at a party, and he wondered if this was the hangover people spoke of. Still, he couldn't shake a strange feeling that was suffocating him. Something didn't feel right. He had been dreaming about an accident. There had been loud noises, people shouting and sirens blaring. He found it difficult to breathe as if his lungs were being crushed.

A throbbing sensation tingled around his head and abdomen. He wasn't in any pain, but he felt uncomfortable. The voices around him began getting more evident, and he could almost make out the voice of his mother. She was asking someone something about his movements. Her voice sounded desperate. Almost terrified. Tyler wondered why she was talking about his movements. He could move, couldn't he? He tried, but he didn't know whether it was working or not.

"Tyler?" An unfamiliar voice penetrated the darkness around him. Tyler wanted to answer, but he couldn't form the words or hear his voice. His throat was sore and dry, as if something was stuck in it. The beeping of a machine seemed to grow louder in his ears.

The composed voice tried again. "Tyler, can you hear me? If you can hear me, can you squeeze my hand?"

Squeeze their hand? Tyler didn't understand. He could feel a warm sensation around his left hand, but he couldn't find the strength to squeeze whatever or whoever it was touching him. He tried, but he just couldn't do it. Fear started to creep up in him, and he wondered what was going on with his body. He felt his eyelids grow lighter as they opened partially, the glare of bright lights piercing him. That reminded him. He had dreamt about bright lights from a torch or a train that was coming straight for him. Tyler pushed the memory away and tried to open his eyes fully even as the familiar voices around him mingled together.

One of the voices said, "It may be gradual, but we will monitor him…"

Who were they monitoring or talking about? His vision was blurry. He was not able to make out the faces of the figures who were right in front of him, and who seemed to be looking down at him. Yet, he could make out the time that was displayed on the digital clock hanging on the wall in front of him. The digits stared back at him. *01:18*. He had seen that time before- just before the bright light had blinded him.

It's just a bad dream, he thought.

His body felt as if it was hit by a freight train. He tried to say something and heard a strange moan slip out of his lips instead. His voice sounded scary, nothing like he knew he sounded.

The unfamiliar voice spoke calmly, saying, "Tyler, you're okay. Just relax. You're in the hospital. We are taking care of you."

In the hospital? Tyler knew he didn't imagine those words. Something horrible had happened. Maybe he did have too much to drink. Perhaps someone had poisoned him. Panic started to erupt inside of him, but the heaviness was back, taking over and forcing his eyes shut. He didn't want to close his eyes again. He needed to wake up.

Something doesn't feel right... something is wrong, he thought. Where was his parents? Where was Noah? Where was Emily?

He felt himself struggle to stay awake, but he lost the battle. His muscles relaxed, and he felt hazy. As he felt himself drift off again, a voice whispered close to his ear.

"Tyler, I'm right here with you. I'm not going to leave you."

A calm crept over him as he was pulled deeper away from the lights, the beeping of machines, and the voices. He didn't recognize or understand much about what was going on. But he would recognize that specific voice anywhere.

It belonged to Emily. His Emmy was there with him.

And if she was there, that meant everything was going to be okay.

Twelve

The warmth from the crackling fire radiated through the living room as Michael turned the page in his Bible to the next chapter.

He was reading the passage on the prodigal son in the book of Luke. The story continuously resonated with Michael over the years, reminding him to have hope that the day would arrive when his son would turn back to God and return home- where he belonged. Month after month and year after year, Michael had wondered when the wait would be over.

Even in the Bible story, the father had a son who had left home, believing he could live his life better on his own terms. The father never went after his son. But he waited patiently each day for the change to come. Then, one day, the son came to his senses, and realized that there was no place like the house of his father. And he returned. It was a compelling story of a son's repentance met with God's grace. Michael was moved by the story because it carried a profound message that nobody was ever too far gone. Even if man gave up on waiting, God never did.

Michael fixed his eyes on a verse that read, *"It was meet that we should make merry, and be glad: for this thy brother was dead, and is alive again, and was lost, and is found."* Michael felt the tears brim his eyes. It was ironic that even in the Word of God, it had been the younger son who had strayed off the right path and who had forgotten who he was- just like Tyler had.

Michael also found it peculiar that the Word of God never revealed the name of the prodigal son. It gave him hope to read it and mentally insert his own son's name in the passage.

He closed the Bible and glanced towards the fire as it hissed. *Was I to blame for failing to recognize my son's struggles?* he thought.

It wasn't the first time a question like that crept into his mind. There were many moments when Michael believed he had not been attentive enough in Tyler's life. He had become so accustomed to recognizing Noah's firm faith that he had failed to see an equal weakness in Tyler's.

Michael remembered warning his younger son about the company and temptations of his youth, but he couldn't recall if he had ever sat Tyler down to answer some of his difficult questions about life. Had he taken it for granted that because they were rooted in the ministry, that his sons were immune from life's attacks?

Michael rubbed his temple. *Were all the teachings and advice from the Word of God for nothing?* he thought. The moment he asked himself the question, a verse jumped out in his spirit. It was a wise saying in the book of Proverbs that said, *Train up a child in the way he should go: and when he is old, he will not depart from it.* Michael smiled, grateful at how the Holy Spirit was able to smooth his anxieties.

He and Beth had done the best they could with both their boys. Tyler was now a grown man, and his choices and walk with God was his responsibility. Michael just hoped it would not be too late before his son turned his life around for good. As a father, all Michael could do was hope and pray.

He let out an exasperated sigh and whispered a prayer saying, *"Lord, what didn't change him in all these years, You can do in these next few days."*

As he ended his prayer, Beth entered the room. She was wearing her white robe and grey bedroom slippers. She came towards him with a cup of his evening tea. Michael took it from her and placed it on the table next to him, still holding onto her hand. "Did our son have anything interesting to say at Dad's place this morning?" he asked her.

Beth closed his hand with her free one and for a short moment, remained quiet before answering, "He asked what we planned on doing with the house. I didn't reply. I didn't want to speak a lie to him by saying that I did not know."

Michael felt a sudden quickening in him. Perhaps if Tyler was asking about the house, he was feeling some kind of curiosity or attachment to it.

That's a good sign, right, Lord? he wondered.

Michael leaned his head back, tired from all his thoughts.

"You did the right thing. I don't know when the right time would be to give him the letter."

Beth sighed and walked to the couch, taking her usual spot on the one end and curling her legs up across the seat next to her. She kept her voice low since Tyler was upstairs. "Is it because you fear what his reaction and decision will be?" Her eyes held a knowing, and Michael knew there was no point in hiding his fears from his wife.

The situation was sensitive. Bill had died, leaving his inheritance and property to Tyler. Ever since Tyler had been a child, he had always reminded his grandfather that the house would one day be his. It had been his dream. It had been Bill's dream to pass it on to his grandsons, too. Michael feared that the news would push Tyler away, causing the house to be sold to another family instead. Beth had always said that one was never to make an impulsive decision on emotions. And Tyler was a master at doing just that.

Beth's voice cut through Michael's concerns. "I can't understand him sometimes. It's as if he is purposefully trying to ruin his life to punish himself." Her voice sounded weak.

Michael ran his hand down the Bible on his lap before speaking. "He is a prisoner to condemnation, Beth. The Bible says that there is no condemnation for those who are in Christ. So, the further he runs from Jesus, the heavier the condemnation will be." He lifted his eyes and met Beth's.

Her face was dejected. She leaned her head against her arm on the sofa, saying, "Noah always had the right things to say to him. If he were here, he would know what to do."

If Noah were here, Tyler wouldn't be in this situation, Michael thought. Instead, he chose to be hopeful. "We will continue praying for a miracle. A divine or supernatural intervention," he said as he leaned his chin on his fist. "God has a future for those who can't even see past today."

He looked back at the fire, believing that miracles were possible. The moment Tyler's eyes had opened in the hospital, they had known they had witnessed a miracle. The doctors had even said so. With minimal recovery and therapy, he was out of the woods quicker than expected. The physical wounds healed, but nothing had prepared them for Tyler's reaction to the news of Noah's death.

Michael's eyes fell on the vibrant orange and red flames dancing together in the fireplace. The heat soothed the chills that were running up his arms from thoughts of that day. When Tyler had gained enough consciousness to know where he was and what had happened, he had asked where Noah was. Although they had dreaded the moment they would have to tell him the truth, they were still unprepared when the moment had arrived. Beth had let out a small cry while squeezing Tyler's hand. She was trying to be brave but was losing that fight. Michael knew it was his responsibility to break the news to his youngest son.

"Tyler didn't make it son," is all he had managed to utter. For a moment, Tyler looked confused, as if he hadn't heard Michael properly. He had blinked a few times, glaring at each of them almost in slow motion. After what felt like a lifetime, the reality of the words seemed to hit him.

Michael squeezed his eyes shut, thinking back to that gut-wrenching moment. He recalled Tyler's face growing stone-cold, the tears silently slipping down his face. They had tried to comfort him, but it was as if an imaginary wall had erected itself around his emotions and heart. Tyler had become a different person in a single moment. The grief and guilt became cemented in him, and he was beside himself. They had also noticed him change towards Emily.

Their vibrant and fun-loving boy had become a stranger.

The sound of footsteps came down the staircase, and Michael and Beth quickly turned their attention to the doorway as Tyler emerged from the corner, dressed casually, and with a jacket in his hand. Michael wondered where he was off to, but he didn't want to sound like the father of a teenager by asking.

Tyler entered the room and looked at Beth, saying, "I'm heading out to the church with the boxes you gave me."

Michael flashed Beth a surprised look. This must have been her doing. She exchanged a guilty look with Michael, but kept her tone light as she turned back to Tyler, replying, "Thank you, Dear. Will you be back early, or do you want a set of keys?"

"I'll take the spare key." And with that, he turned to leave.

When Michael heard the front door lock, he studied Beth. She had a deliberately composed look on her face. Michael let out a light chuckle and asked, "Are you in the match-making business now? I don't think Ian would be too pleased with your antics."

Beth rolled her eyes with the hint of a smile. Her voice was detached as if she were not guilty of his implied accusation. "I don't know what you mean, Michael. I thought it would do him good seeing what Emily has done with the youth at church." She fiddled with her gown and looked at him. "Besides, what is meant to be will be."

Michael understood what his wife meant. He knew that Beth did not have a single malicious or meddling bone in her body. She would never try to use Tyler to cause a wedge between Ian and Emily. Emily was like a daughter to them. And ever since Emily's parents had relocated out of town years prior, Beth and Michael had always been more active in her life so that she didn't feel the absence of her family. They would never want to hurt her.

"We always believed and prayed that Emily was the one for Tyler." Beth's voice was reflective. Michael didn't disagree. He, too, had looked forward to the season when Tyler and Emily married. He believed they would have been a pillar couple in the ministry and would have raised a family just down the road from him and Beth.

But now, in light of everything that had happened, he felt a little differently. Michael knew that if he did have a daughter, he would want his daughter to marry a man that loved the Lord, who would lead her, protect her heart, and raise their children in the ways of the Word. He would want her to be with a man who was mature and reliable. One who could give her a stable home and family of their own.

As much as Michael's heart desired Tyler and Emily to find their way back together, he couldn't help but believe that at that moment, Tyler was not the suitable choice for Emily.

"Mike, there's something I always wondered." Beth's voice was soft. Michael focused his attention back on her. Her eyes were fixed on his as she continued. "When Tyler first left home, we always believed he would return after graduation. But he never did. For twelve years, we have waited." She sighed. "Now he's here. Why have we never just asked him to come back home?"

Michael felt the lump in his throat. He let his eyes fall to his Bible and remembered the story of the prodigal son.

His voice was a whisper when he answered his wife. "Because when a son leaves home on his own, he will need to return on his own."

Thirteen

The youth meeting drew a large group of the regular teen-agers. A few new faces had strolled in halfway through the session, and Emily had greeted them with excitement. It made her heart swell to know that there were youngsters who preferred to be in the church on a Friday night discussing things about God, rather than being out in the world. Emily was glad to be an instrument in what God was doing in their lives.

"Okay, everyone! Let's bring our chairs together to form a circle so that we can get to the next activity." Emily waved a few of the scattered teens towards her and waited as they shuffled about, dragging chairs across the floor and racing to find their spots next to their close friends.

The group was always excited about the activity she had planned, as it usually held a profound spiritual message that they could learn from whilst having fun. The activity she had planned for that evening was something that she needed to practice more of- especially after her rollercoaster week of emotions.

Emily was just about to take her seat when a figure walked in through the back doors and paused momentarily. Emily's heart fluttered.

It was Tyler. His eyes caught hers, and he lifted his hand with a small acknowledging wave. Some of the other teenagers looked towards him and then back at Emily.

One of the teenagers spoke up. "Em, that's Pastor Mike's son."

Emily smiled at the teen. "Yes, I know. Let me see if he wants to join us." She excused herself from the group and made her way towards Tyler. He had his hands shoved in his pockets and wore a pleasant smile on his face.

He spoke as she drew nearer to him. "I just came by to drop off some boxes. I've left them in the storeroom." He motioned with his thumb over his shoulder to the room. Emily could smell his scent from where she stood, and she felt the butterflies awaken. She looked over her shoulder at the group, who were now waiting on her. Their voices in hushed tones while settling down.

She played with her hands in front of her as she asked him, "Would you like to join us? We are about to participate in a group activity." She saw his eyes move from the crowd of teenagers back to hers, hesitantly. She chuckled, trying to lighten the mood. "Come on. We won't Bible punch you. You can just listen if you want."

Tyler let out a light chuckle and rubbed his jaw with his hand before giving in, saying, "Okay, only for a little while."

Emily felt something leap inside of her. They walked back

to the group together as the teenagers focused their attention on Tyler. Emily smiled at the group as she did the introduction. "Everyone, this is Tyler. He is Pastor Mike and Mrs. Hill's son. And he's here to make sure that I am teaching you guys something worthwhile!" Her voice was teasing, and a choir of laughter echoed around the circle. A smile worked it's way across Tyler's face as he greeted the group and took his place on one of the empty seats. Emily noticed a few of the teenage girls giggle shyly at the sight of him.

She found her spot a few seats away but was still within a clear view of him. She clasped her hands in front of her. "So today, we are going to play a some-what encouraging game called *Treasures In Darkness.*" She saw the eyes of many of the youngsters light up. There were also some gasps of excitement that resonated around the circle. She couldn't help but notice the nervousness on Tyler's face. He was not in his comfort zone, but she soldiered ahead.

"So, the Bible says in Isaiah 45:3 that God will give us treasures that are hidden in dark places, and that He will give us riches from the secret places."

She took a breath and held the gaze of each teenager before continuing. "Sometimes, in our dark moments, we cannot see what good can come from it. But there is always something precious that God wants to teach us or some kind of blessing He wants to bring forth from the dark time if we just listen and let Him."

The teenagers were captivated, their eyes locked on hers, agreeing with nods and deep thoughts. Some even scribbled some notes in their notebooks. Emily watched Tyler shift uncomfortably in his seat, and she wondered if he would change his mind and leave.

She decided to stay focused on the task at hand. "Think about a caterpillar in a cocoon. It must be a dark and confusing time for the little creature. But then, suddenly, in a single moment-" she put her hands out and widened her eyes, "it breaks forth as a butterfly."

"A new creation!" One of the teenagers piped up.

Emily nodded. "And we are all new creations in Christ Jesus!"

A few *wows* and *Amen's* resounded.

Emily clasped her hands together, saying, "So, tonight, each of us needs to think about something confusing that happened in our lives and find the blessing that was hidden within. We are going to find the gratitude despite that dark season."

Expressions of anticipation and excitement flashed on many of the teenagers' faces. Tyler had his arms folded casually but looked pensive. Emily was not planning on putting him on the spot to engage with everyone on the topic. She knew that he wasn't in a place in his life to find the blessing in anything. She just wanted him to witness the good that was being planted in each of the youngsters, and she silently prayed that something would impact his spirit.

Emily tucked her hair behind her ear and scanned the circle of faces around her. "So, who would like to go first?"

There were some giggles, some awkward silences, and even a few witty teens who were raising the hands of the friends sitting next to them.

One of the teenagers spoke up, saying, "Emily, why don't you go first and give us a head start as an example?"

Emily nodded. "Okay, that's a good idea." She thought for a moment and then spoke intently. "When I was planning to open my coffee shop a few years ago, I had my heart set on this perfect little space on Green Street. It was just opposite the shopping mall-"

"Yes, I know that spot!" One of the teenagers interrupted. "It's now taken over by some real estate agents."

Emily smiled. "Exactly. When they signed the papers before I could decide on the space, I was devastated." She paused for a moment. "I developed all these emotions of fear and anxiety that my dream was not going to come to pass the way I had hoped." She gazed intently at everyone; all were hanging onto her every word.

"Then, my current coffee shop space became available. It was in a much better location and for a much more reasonable price!" She threw her hands up, delight in her voice, explaining, "The burden set me up for an unexpected blessing! God had a better treasure in store for me. So, I am grateful that it worked out for my good."

Several *Amen's* and applause went around the room even as one teen spoke up, saying, "And, we are all grateful for your pancakes, Emily!"

Other teenagers were laughing and returning the compliment. Emily noticed Tyler's eyes fixed on her, a slight smile on his face. She felt the warmth creep into her neck and she hoped he would not notice.

He's looking at me like that again, she thought. It was a look of adoration, one that made her want to travel back in time to nineteen when all was picture perfect, and the colors on their canvas of life were bright and promising.

She forced a smile and looked at a group of teens. "Okay, Serena, why don't you try?"

The teenager squeezed her hands together and leaned forward, looking nervous. Her voice was shy when she spoke. "I struggled with moving schools a few months ago and leaving all of my friends who I had grown up with." She shrugged. "I really felt like my parents were unfair to do that to me. But I guess I have found a treasure in that situation because if I hadn't moved schools, I wouldn't have met Amy who became the greatest friend I've ever had." Serena looked over at her friend Amy, and the two shared a side hug. Serena grinned while saying, "So, I'm grateful for new friendships."

"I'll go next!" A freckle-faced red-head put his hand up, eager to share his burden and blessing. His other arm was wrapped in a sling around his neck.

Emily nodded at him, "Go for it, Tim."

He pointed at his compromised arm with his free one. "I broke my arm while playing with my cousins a few weeks ago. The injury made me miss a few tennis matches," his face dropped, "Which I was pretty bummed about." He took a breath and continued. "But the blessing in that is that I still have my arm, and it's going to heal so I can get back out there on the court, you know?"

There were some claps and hoots from around the group, and Tim shrugged. "Some people lose their limbs in worse accidents and can never play their favorite sport again. So I'm grateful that it will heal in time. That's my treasure."

Emily felt her heart swell. The teenagers were grasping the importance of being grateful for the blessings in their lives, even through the darkest of times. It would be something that would echo through their lives later on, even if they didn't realize it now.

They spent the next hour going through each person's treasures in darkness. When they had finished with the last teenager, Emily leaned forward, saying, "Okay, well, that's it for tonight. Let's close with a prayer before our snacks arrive."

One of the regular teenagers spoke up quickly. "Emily, we haven't finished with everyone."

Emily frowned and quickly scanned the group of teens. She was pretty sure she hadn't left anyone out. The teenager motioned at Tyler, while saying, "Tyler hasn't had a chance to go yet."

Emily felt a pit in her stomach. It wasn't her intention to make Tyler feel uncomfortable, but the other teens had no clue about him or his life to have known better. Emily couldn't blame them.

Tyler's face had been focused on each teenager as they told their stories. Emily watched the apprehension enter his features as he leaned forward, clearly being put on the spot but not wanting to dampen the evening. She wondered what he would say, or if she was to step in and excuse him from participating.

Before she could decide, he spoke, to her surprise.

His voice was collected. "Well, my grandfather passed away this week, as many of you would know." He placed his palms together in a nervous manner and shrugged, saying, "So, the burden would have to be me coming back to his funeral and dealing with that."

Before he could continue, another teenager interjected, "That's horrible! What could be the blessing in that?"

"He's getting to that, be quiet!" Another boy scowled at his friend.

Everyone's attention was back on Tyler. The youngsters seemed quite taken with him. Tyler's eyes met Emily's, and the lump in her throat was back as he answered the group.

"The blessing is that I got the chance to see a good friend again, after many years." He smiled before continuing. "And I'm grateful for that. I'm grateful for her."

Being at the youth meeting brought on a surge of emotions within him, even though all he had done was listen in silence. When none of the teenagers were paying him much attention after their activities, Tyler slipped out the front doors of the church.

He strolled down the pavement towards the grassy area. A cool breeze circulated the air. He pulled his jacket closer around him and walked towards the bench at the edge of the pond. It had been years since he had sat on the bench. It was a place that held hours of in-depth conversations with Emily when they were younger.

The teenagers at the meeting were inspiring. He couldn't dispute that. Tyler knew that Noah would have been so pleased with what Emily had done with the group. And she did it so well, even on her own. Every word that she spoke captivated him and chiseled away at something in his heart.

The teenagers were roaring with laughter inside the church. Tyler looked over his shoulder and caught a glimpse of Emily through the glass doors. She was busy organizing the pizza and sodas for the socializing part of the evening. He saw her throw her head back, laughing, and his stomach curled at the sight. When he was a teenager, he hadn't realized that there was a clean and safe way of having fun with friends- much like Emily was doing with the youth of the church. If he had known, he wouldn't have tried so hard to fit in with Ricky and his friends; a mistake that had initiated all the pain and loss that night.

Crickets chirped nearby, and he broke his eyes off of her and leaned his head back against the bench and looked up. Numerous stars glistened across the dark blanket of the night sky. It was a beautiful sight. *Treasures in darkness,* he thought. So much in that message had moved him.

He hadn't meant to catch Emily off guard when he had shared that he was grateful for her. But it was the truth. Coming back had been difficult. But seeing her was the only treasure he could think of. For years, a gaping hole had taken root in the secret places of his heart because of what he had done to her. Seeing her successful, and walking in her purpose in the ministry made the hole inside of him knit together. He was happy that she had found some meaning in her life even though he knew he could not share it with her as they had once planned together.

The sound of crunching leaves caught his attention. He looked over his shoulder and saw Emily approaching. Their eyes met briefly, and he smiled, patting the empty spot beside him on the bench. It was the place she would have willingly taken years ago without him even having to ask. He saw the apprehension cross her face, but she made her way around the bench and lowered herself to it. She was careful not to sit too close to him.

Smart girl, he thought.

She followed his gaze to the sky above, and he saw a look of wonder flash across her features. She spoke, her expression dream-like, saying, "The Bible says we should lift our eyes to the heavens. He's the One who brings out the stars one by one and calls them by name." She smiled, her eyes fixed on the sparkling stars above them.

Tyler followed her gaze. "You believe the stars have names?", he asked doubtfully.

She nodded without hesitation. "If the Bible says it, I believe it." She kept her voice low, continuing, "And it says that not one of them is missing or forgotten."

Tyler felt a chill run down his neck. He had heard something similar from his grandfather many years ago.

So much is missing and forgotten, Emily, he thought.

He was about to change the subject when she did instead. "The kids liked having you here tonight. You're really good with them."

Tyler couldn't help but flash her a teasing smile as he turned towards her. "Just the kids?" He noticed that she didn't return the banter as she usually would. He wondered if he had gone too far or if his tone had been too flirty. It was difficult remembering that she belonged to someone else.

A light breeze wafted past, and he watched as she hugged her arms around herself. Tyler couldn't help but smile. He leaned forward, swinging his jacket off of him. He held it out to her, saying, "Here."

The color crept into her cheeks when she met his eyes. "No, it's okay. I'm fine."

Tyler chuckled lightly. "It won't bite, Emily." He laughed. "Although, you still have one of my favorite jackets from years ago that you haven't returned."

His words triggered an unusual look on her face, as if she was thinking back to that night. She paused before taking his jacket from his hands. She threw it around her shoulders, and untucked her hair from inside the collar.

A drawn out, frozen moment of silence followed. Tyler felt a lump in his throat. It was like déjà vu.

He leaned back in his spot, folding his arms against himself. It took a moment for his body to adjust to the cold. The wind rustled the leaves across the grass as they both gazed at the sky above them. Tyler watched her closely from the corner of his eye. There were far too many lines that could not be crossed, no matter how much he ached to cross them. Especially now under the glare of the moonlight on her face, every inch of him wanted to move closer as if time and circumstances hadn't separated them.

Even twelve years later, she was the only one who moved him to feel that way. He let his eyes wander to the ring on her finger and felt the muscle in his jaw flex, remembering his place.

"Dad said your wedding is in a few months," he said casually.

His comment certainly got her attention. Her eyes broke away from the stars and she looked expressionless as she angled to face him. She dropped her palms to the bench to support herself.

"Yes, in twenty weeks, to be exact." The teasing look he was familiar with found her face again as she said, "I would invite you to the wedding, but I doubt this town will ever see you again once you leave this time." She let out a single but sarcastic laugh. "Besides, I don't think family gatherings, love, and celebrations are quite your scene anymore."

Although her comment hit its mark, Tyler recognized the hurt in her voice, and sensed her many questions. She was trying so hard not to reveal the pain he had caused her. But he saw it. It was written in every look she gave him. It was hidden in every sarcastic comment she made.

He needed to make her understand, but he didn't know how to do it. There were so many words on the tip of his tongue that he was afraid would stumble out.

Before he could even stop himself, he looked at her bare hand resting on the space next to him, and he reached for it, covering hers with his. It was the first time they were skin to skin since their goodbye at the airport twelve years ago. Something about the moment created a pit in his stomach. He welcomed the sensation of her hand under his after all this time, realizing how much he had missed her.

Emily stared at his hand momentarily and slowly raised her eyes to search his. The flecks of green he was so drawn to glistened in the glare of the moonlight and stars. She didn't pull her hand away, and he was grateful for that.

Tyler swallowed. He needed to seize the moment and say it now, or he didn't think he ever would. He let his words out carefully.

"Emmy, I'm sorry."

He met her gaze again and hesitated before plunging ahead with what he wanted to say all day long. Or, maybe it was what he had wanted to say for years. He felt the lump in his throat grow thicker as he said, "I never meant to hurt you. You have to believe me."

In an instant, the sadness in her eyes changed to something else- indignation. She pulled her hand out from under his as if he had touched her with burning coals. She raised her eyebrows at him, as if he were a stranger. He was taken aback by her sudden attitude change.

Her icy stare was back, and her tone fierce when she spat out her words. "Really?" Her voice dripped with a touch of derision he had never heard from her before. He was about to interject to explain himself when she continued, her eyes burning holes into his.

"You never meant to hurt me?" She took a loud breath, dramatic almost. "Okay, Tyler, how did you think I was going to feel?"

She pulled her arms across her chest as a mother would do for her spoiled toddler, waiting for his excuse.

Tyler leaned forward, wishing that he could take the last few moments back and not have gone there. Perhaps silence had been the better option. But he owed her this much now that they were waist-deep in bitter waters. He planted his elbows on his knees and rubbed either side of his temple with his fingertips.

He kept his tone even. "Emily, you wouldn't understand what I was going through. I thought it was the right thing for both of us."

She barely let him get through the last word before she stood to her feet abruptly. He had unleashed her wrath. Her feisty nature that he had remembered as a teenager was even gutsier now.

She looked down at him, her eyes brimming with tears. "Well, you were wrong!" She pointed her finger at him as she went on. "And you don't get to tell me that I wouldn't understand. That wasn't just your decision to make!" Her voice grew louder as her hand dropped to her side. "I needed you! Your parents also needed you! And now, twelve years later, you think just saying *sorry* heals it all?" She threw her hands in the air, asking, "What are you sorry for, Tyler?"

She eyed him like a bug as she rapidly fired questions at him, giving him no chance to reply. "Running away? Forgetting your parents and their loss? Breaking my heart? Ruining our future plans? Becoming a complete jerk- someone I barely recognize? If it wasn't for Uncle Bill's funeral, would you even be here saying you are sorry?"

Every word she said was like a knife twisting into his gut. Emotion filled him as he saw the hurt etched across her face. But at the same time, he felt his own frustrations start to bubble. He understood that she was heartbroken and confused, but nobody seemed to understand his position. How was he to describe the guilt and loss that daily consumed him? Nobody could have helped him, because there was no help possible for what he had done and what he was struggling with.

She was right in everything she had asked. Time did not heal all wounds. And she had deserved more than a text message. Letting her go was one of the most grueling decisions he had ever made. But, it was the right thing to do because she deserved more than what he could give her. He would not have made her happy when he himself was no longer the same person she had known.

He leaned back against the bench and stared at her blankly, wishing she would understand him this one time. His voice pleaded with her as he replied, saying, "Emmy, I just needed to be left alone."

"For twelve years?" She fired back, unrelenting. She lost the battle with her emotions as a single teardrop rolled down her face. She wiped it away angrily, like she would swat a gnat. He hated it when she cried. He wanted to go to her, but her face made him realize it was best he stayed away.

Her voice cracked. "Well, you know what, Tyler?" She cocked her head to the side as she spoke through gritted teeth. "It sure didn't look like you wanted to be left alone in the parking lot of your college the day I saw you."

Tyler felt the earth tremble beneath him at her words. He felt his throat constrict, and his brows furrowed together as he searched her face. He could only make out a simple question, the heat pouring into him.

"What?" He rose slowly to his feet, asking again, "What day are you talking about?" He couldn't help but hear the quiver in his voice, afraid of what her answer may be.

A deafening silence hung between them until she spoke, much softer this time, explaining, "I came to find you. A year after you had left and sent me that text."

Tyler felt the ground spinning. Nobody had told him that. But, how would he have known after effectively shutting them all out of his life?

Emily let her hands fall to her side. She seemed to have gathered her emotions before she spoke again. "I just wanted to find you and tell you that I'm there for you." She paused for a moment. "And that I would wait for you."

Tyler felt sick. A nausea rose within him and he felt light-headed. Had she really been prepared to wait for him?

"I did see you." Her face looked pained as those words escaped her lips. Tyler knew that she chose to stop right there, without describing the events she had truly witnessed. He was silently relieved that she didn't explain any further. He already felt like the worst person in the world. He couldn't remember the exact date she was referring to, but he remembered the kind of activities he got up to in college, especially in the parking lot.

He shuddered at the thought.

She had come to find him and had left even more heartbroken than before.

Tyler fought the urge to go to her and envelop her in his arms, begging her to forgive him. It was so much easier being away from her all these years and not truly seeing the effect his actions had caused in her heart. But standing in front of her and witnessing the heartbreak painted on her face made him hate himself even more.

If that's even possible, he wondered.

She sniffed and wiped the base of her palm across her nose. When her eyes found him, he saw the yearning within them. She lowered her gaze, battling with her defeated emotions. "I just need to know one thing. If I never know anything else, it's fine. Just tell me one thing..."

The atmosphere between them became electric. Tyler held his breath, and steadied himself. There was so much he wanted to tell her. She studied his face a long while, and he noticed her lower lip tremble. She gained control of herself before she asked a question that took his breath away.

"Did you blame me for Noah's death? Is that why you left me?" She sighed, her eyes glassy with tears. "Is that what broke us?"

Tyler remembered the impact of the truck on his vehicle years ago. This felt almost similar; a sledgehammer to his heart.

Before he knew it, and without caring for the consequences, he closed the gap between them and took a firm grip of either side of her arms. She seemed so small beneath his touch. Her shoulders drooped, and it wasn't from the weight of his jacket around her. Their faces were so close together that he could smell the vanilla scent of the shampoo in her hair.

His words were a struggle. "Emmy, listen to me." He moved his hands from her arms to either side of her face. Her doe-eyes were wide and wounded, pools of tears overwhelming them. He knew that she had been carrying that question within her for twelve years. And his silence over that time had allowed it to fester in her heart like a disease.

Of course, she had felt to blame. She was the one who had phoned Noah to pick him up when he was drunk. He needed her to know the truth.

He rested his forehead against hers, closing his eyes for a moment. He could almost feel the despair radiating from her through his fingertips. She didn't push him away. Instead, her eyes searched his, desperate for an answer as if she were waiting for this moment her whole life.

Tyler let out a breath, his hands never leaving either side of her face. He wanted to answer her with a kiss- one that would tell her how he truly felt about her. But he managed to steel himself from doing that.

He nuzzled his face against her hair. And his voice was wounded when he answered her. "You were not to blame for anything that happened that night." He said each word deliberately and with no room for misinterpretation. "Whatever broke was because of me…" He took a breath, as her green eyes soaked him in.

He whispered once more, "Everything that went wrong was because of me."

Fourteen

12 years before...

The headstone was simple, much like Noah had been.

Tyler stared at the light grey slab with its intricate design around the border. A cross engraved the center, and Noah's name, date of birth, and date of death were underneath.

Noah had only been twenty-five years old. The words IN LOVING MEMORY OF A WONDERFUL SON AND DEVOTED BROTHER-GOODBYE FOR NOW were printed across the center. It was true. Noah had been both- right to the very end.

Tyler's loss felt impossible to come to terms with. One moment coupled with his foolishness, had changed everything. The pain was now woven with his guilt and regret.

The wind rustled the leaves in the trees, causing a few to glide to the ground. Tyler's eyes took in the bouquets, and single white stemmed roses left around the headstone and on the grass near his feet. Eventually, the flowers would wilt, and the headstone would fade, but the ache would remain. The people who had sympathized with their family's tragedy would move on with their lives, yet Tyler and his parents would forever have a void within them and a chasm between them.

From the time he had found out about Noah's death, Tyler felt as if something switched off inside of him. He was angry and didn't see the point of anything in life.

His eyes fell to a candle in a jar that was left to the side of the headstone. Even the flame had been snuffed out, mirroring what he had done to his own brother's life.

The heartbreak suffocated him. It was almost unbearable. He couldn't eat. He couldn't sleep. He even despised his reflection. Every morning that he opened his eyes, he hoped that it had all been a terrible nightmare. Tyler hoped to hear Noah's voice from downstairs, or see him getting ready to head out for a meeting or to work.

Tyler choked back the cry within him. *How did I let this happen? It should have been me*, he thought.

He remembered Ricky's words. *"What's the big deal? You're not going to hell for one drink."*

Tyler clenched his fists. *This sure feels like hell*, he thought.

It had been just over three months since the accident happened. The doctors called Tyler's recovery and bill of health a miracle. His parents had shared his recovery as a testimony at church. They even thanked everyone for their prayers. Tyler was grateful he hadn't been to church since. The last thing he wanted to do was sit in church and hear what a miracle he was when nobody could answer a simple question: Why had God failed to save Noah?

Tyler didn't feel there was anything to be thankful for. He didn't believe it was a miracle to have made it out of that wreck alive. He believed it was his punishment. He had disregarded in-struction, he had broken promises, and had welcomed the temp-tation with open arms. And now, his brother was gone.

Because of him.

He leaned his head back and looked at the dark sky above him, the clouds rolling together. The weather reports said that it was going to storm later on. Tyler felt his own storm raging inside of him. If God had wanted to punish him for his foolish decisions that one night, He should have spared Noah's life and taken him instead. Noah had said that every action had consequences. Tyler realized living with the guilt was going to be his.

He remembered seeing an article that was printed in the local newspaper about the accident. His father had forgotten to get rid of it by the time Tyler was discharged from the hospital.

It had said *Local Pastor's Sons In Fatal Car Accident.*

It had even mentioned that the sole cause of the collision was a truck driver who thought he could make the red light just as Tyler and Noah had entered the intersection. Tyler knew that the article had it all wrong. The sole cause of the collision was not the truck. It had been him. If he had not made poor choices, his brother would never have been in the car with him at that intersection at that time. If he had just gone home or avoided the party altogether, Noah would not have been in the middle of giving Tyler a lecture on his poor choices, seconds before he was killed.

So many *what if's* and *why's* consumed him.

Tyler lowered his head and sucked in a breath. All Noah's advice that night was for nothing. Noah had lived his life according to the handbook of God, and it had not been enough to save him. Tyler wondered what the point in having faith was if his own brother hadn't benefitted from it.

He stared at his brother's name on the headstone.

"Noah, what would you say to me now? Where was your God when you needed Him?" His voice was barely a whisper. The tears stung the corner of his eyes. He wished with everything in him that Noah would come back and speak to him again; to tell him what to do.

A rustling caught him off guard. Tyler looked up and noticed an older man sweeping the leaves from around some of the graves. The man caught his gaze and smiled at Tyler. His eyes were soft and kind, some wrinkles around his cheeks. He was probably one of the graveyard workers. Tyler didn't know how a person was able to be around so much death and loss and yet still have such a pleasant smile across his face. The man drew closer, and Tyler felt uncomfortable at his nearness. All he wanted was to be alone with his brother for a few moments before his flight left to a new city where he would try to start his life over.

Doctors called it post-traumatic stress disorder. Tyler knew it as another word.

Guilt.

Even Emily couldn't understand why he wanted to move away. He remembered her words. *"The pain is not going to be any different there than it is here. Please stay."*

He hadn't wanted to argue with her, but she wouldn't understand. He knew the pain would not disappear, but he could no longer bear the grief on his parents' faces any longer. He couldn't take the quiet bedroom next to his. He couldn't stand to see the empty chair at dinner. He wouldn't be able to avoid the disapproving eyes and gossiping whispers of the church folk every time he walked into a room. He couldn't drive past the scene of the accident and ever be okay again. He wouldn't be able to look at a single person who was at that party that night and not feel as if he were right back there, being foolish and disobedient. He needed to leave home. It was the only way he could try to face himself in time.

Tyler shifted his weight to his other leg, wincing at the slight tingle of pain around his middle. The doctors had said that in time, he would be as good as new. That was the biggest lie Tyler had ever heard. He could never be new. The physical scars were nothing compared to the ones he harbored within.

The rustling of the footsteps grew closer.

"Noah was a faithful and favored man in the eyes of the Lord." The graveyard worker's voice caught Tyler's attention.

Tyler frowned at the man as an unexpected lump lodged itself in his throat. The man was wearing a khaki-colored jumpsuit with the name tag *"Gabe"* across the side. What had he said about Noah?

How did he know Noah?

The man smiled politely and rested his hands on the top of the broom. He seemed to have sensed Tyler's questions. He continued, saying, "In the Bible. The earth was corrupted, so the Lord chose Noah to build the ark before the flood came. I see his name is Noah too." He pointed at the headstone.

"Yes, I know the story!" Tyler quipped. He didn't care that his response dripped with irritation. He didn't want to be reminded about Bible stories at this time.

The man's pleasant face prevailed as he cocked his head to the side, eyeing Tyler. "Good. Then you should know the meaning of the story."

Tyler kept his tone cheeky, hoping the man would pick up on it and leave. "Yes, I know the meaning of the story too." He let out a huff as he continued, "God punished the earth for their wrongs and wiped them out. But He saved Noah and his family in the ark."

Tyler felt fresh tears brim his eyes as he stared at his brother's headstone. Even in the Bible, Noah had been a good man, much like his own brother had been.

He gritted his teeth and looked at the man defiantly, saying, "But reality is much different, Sir. It's not some Bible story we can read and put our hope in." He let his eyes fall to the headstone again. "In reality, God doesn't keep His word. Not even to those who are faithful to Him."

An unexpected tear rolled out of his eye, and Tyler wiped it away with his fist. He spoke through gritted teeth. "The one who wholeheartedly loved Him, and who always encouraged people to believe in Him and live righteously is now dead. But the one who did the wrong and who had doubts about this whole faith-thing is alive instead. What kind of God allows that to happen?"

He felt angry that he was even having some useless conversation with a stranger about God and faith. If he wanted to be Bible punched, he would have gone to his parents or Emily at this time. They were the ones continuously talking about God's plans and all the promises in the Bible, promises that even Noah had believed in but had not lived to see or fulfill. Tyler didn't want to hear anything about God. In his opinion, having faith was for the weak. It prevented them from facing the reality of their situations and actions.

The man walked closer, his eyes falling to the flowers around the headstone. He reached out and put a hand on Tyler's shoulder. Tyler instantly felt an unfamiliar warmth around his body at the man's touch. He had a fatherly way about him. Ordinarily, Tyler would have shrugged the man off. He didn't know the stranger well enough to be touched by him. But something about the man's disposition brought Tyler a little comfort. For a moment, it felt as if the man was the first person to understand his pain.

The man's voice was loving when he spoke, saying, "Tyler, you're focusing so much on the message of the flood, that you've forgotten the message of the rainbow."

Tyler frowned, confused. What was this man on about? Before he could ask, the man stepped aside and started whistling as he walked away. Tyler watched him go and felt the icy breeze come over his body again. The entire exchange was so bizarre that Tyler brushed it aside. He focused back on his brother's grave and dropped down in a hunkering position.

He reached out and touched Noah's name on the grey block. A lump formed in his throat. He wanted to say one last thing, but he didn't know what. The words wouldn't form. It felt similar to when he was in the coma and couldn't break out of the deep sleep no matter how hard he tried. Tyler sniffed and squeezed his eyes shut. The last thing he had wanted to say in the car to Noah was that he was sorry for the events of that evening. He had barely got the apology out when the truck had hit them. And now, even as he stared at the headstone, Tyler realized his words were still the same.

He let out a small whisper. "I'm sorry, Noah. This was all my fault."

He knew that saying sorry didn't change anything. It didn't bring Noah back, and it wouldn't move the heart of God to make this all a bad dream. But it was the only thing he had left to give his brother- an apology.

He stood up and dusted his fingers on his jeans. He heard a deep rumble in the sky from the storm that would be rolling in sooner than he expected. He hoped his flight wouldn't be canceled because of it. He needed to leave as quickly as possible. He couldn't bare staying any longer.

He made his way towards his father's car, which was parked on the hill above. As he looked back at the countless graves, his eyes fell on Noah's once more. It was sitting idyllically underneath one of the large trees, sheltered and peaceful. Tyler captured a mental photo because he knew he would never be back to revisit it.

He promised himself that he would not come back at all.

The face of the man who Tyler had spoken to earlier flashed before him.

Gabe, was it? Tyler thought.

He couldn't help but scope the grounds for the stranger again. The man had left Tyler with some confusion about floods and rainbows. What had he said? That Tyler was focusing so much on the message of the flood that he had forgotten the message of the rainbow?

What rainbow? Tyler thought. He held the steering wheel of the car and let his eyes scan the area again, even looking up at the sky for a possible rainbow. He shook his head, annoyed.

That's when something strange hit him.

How had the stranger known his name?

Emily had been staring blankly at the same page in her textbook for an hour. Thoughts of Tyler and his relocation swirled in her head, making it difficult to concentrate. He had left for a new city and college a week ago, and already, Emily felt like they had grown worlds apart. Things felt tense. It was as if they were forced to check in with one another, and to carry a meaningful conversation. Most of the time, it was her initiating the conversation. Still, Tyler did not seem emotionally present.

She wanted to give him space and support after the loss of his brother, but didn't know how best to do it. It was one thing to comfort someone who had lost a loved one. It was another thing to comfort someone who blamed themselves for that loss.

A few students were chuckling behind the bookshelves in the library, and Emily watched as one of the library clerks hushed them down and pointed to the exit. The sheepish students scurried off, books in their hands.

Emily sighed. A few months ago, she and Tyler had known the feeling of easy-going laughter and fun. Now, their lives had all taken a dramatic turn. Every time she spoke to him, she felt as if she were walking on eggshells. She recalled an evening when she had asked him if she could say a prayer with him, and he had cut her off bluntly, saying he wasn't in the mood for prayer. That concerned her. He was struggling with his faith even more since the accident.

Emily propped her elbow on the table and leaned her face against her closed fist. The textbook stared back at her. The day that he had left for the airport should have given her an indication of what it would be like once he was gone. He had been distant since returning from Noah's grave. She had offered to go with him, but he had abruptly declined.

The drive to the airport with his family had been worse. Nobody had said anything significant. Whenever his mother or father had tried to comment on his new apartment or his college electives, he would keep his replies short, leaving no room for conversation. He hadn't even noticed his mother wiping at her stray tears in the passenger seat.

After embracing his parents for a long while at the departure gates, he had stood in front of her. For the first time in months, he had finally looked at her and not through her. In a split moment, it felt as if they were them again—the old Tyler and Emily. Emily had tried her best not to cry. She hadn't wanted to make the moment about her, but the truth was that her heart was in pieces. She had grown up with Tyler being a few roads away from her, and she had no clue what his relocation was going to mean for their future together.

She had believed that an engagement would have followed graduation and that they would have started planning their lives together. That's all they had ever spoken about- the future. Now, that beautiful picture of plans that they had clicked together seemed ruined and hanging in mid-air.

His words had been careful with her at the airport. "I'll text you when I land."

Emily had held his gaze, saying, "I'm going to miss you. But we'll visit each other at least once every few weeks, right?"

Her tone had been desperate, but she knew that distance was no match for how they felt about one another. Besides, if Tyler never returned home, Emily was prepared to leave town after graduation and start their lives wherever he felt at peace. She loved him enough to do that for him.

Tyler had broken her gaze and had weaved his fingers between hers, his head kept down. Emily had felt her heart quicken and wondered why he wasn't doing everything in his power to convince her that all was well between them. He always eased her anxieties before. He always protected her heart.

"Right." His voice had been flat, his dark eyes drawing away from her. Emily had wanted to shake him and ask him why he was doing this to her. She needed more than this. She desperately needed the words he had told her on the night of the party- that she was the only thing he was ever sure of. Now, he was behaving like a stranger.

Before Emily could say anything, he had pulled her in for a hug, but the warmth of it was lost. His hand had been on the back of her head, and she had felt his breath on her neck. He had stayed that way for a long time, and Emily had felt moisture on her shoulder. She had gulped back her tears and had clung onto him, wondering if it would make him stay.

After a few moments, he had pulled back, his eyes pink and glassy. He had picked up his backpack, slinging it over his shoulder, giving his father and mother another hug each. Their faces looked just as broken as Emily's heart must-have. As he was about to leave, Emily had forced a smile. She desired one moment of normalcy between them. Her voice fought through the pain.

"Hey, Tyler…"

He had turned and searched her face. Waiting.

She kept her tone light. "You didn't say it…"

He knew what she had meant. The corner of his mouth lifted slightly, and when he spoke, his tone held a depth to it she had never heard from him before.

"Don't forget me, Emmy…"

Emily let out a sigh of relief. Her name on his lips always revealed his true feelings for her. She hugged herself as she managed to find her voice, replying, "Never…"

They had watched him walk through the departure gates and to the security line. Emily waited for him to turn around and flash them a goodbye smile, or even a final wave. He didn't do either. He slowly blended into the crowd of other passengers until they couldn't see him anymore. Emily allowed the hot tears to stream down her face. She had been holding them at bay for too long.

Beth had found her place next to her and had put her arm around her shoulders, still looking ahead.

Emily turned and searched her face, saying, "Beth, that felt like a forever goodbye."

Beth didn't disagree with her, and her lip trembled as she looked over at her husband, whose eyes brimmed with tears.

"Excuse me, is this seat taken?"

The voice interrupted Emily's memory, and she looked up at another student who was motioning at the chair next to her. Emily smiled at the girl and said no, moving her things off the table so the student could sit down. She took a glimpse at her phone and noticed a text message had come through.

Her heart quickened. It was from Tyler. He was probably free to chat with her now. She opened the text message but felt the air leave her lungs a few seconds into it. Her heart started to cave in.

Emmy. I've been thinking a lot this week. This is not fair for both of us. Things will never be as they once were. It's best we go our separate ways.

Please don't call or text. Move on with your life. I have with mine. I'm sorry for doing this now and like this. It's just better this way. Goodbye.

Emily felt her fingers shake as she scrolled through the message again. He was joking, wasn't he? How had he gone from saying things wouldn't change between them to now saying they were over?

Emily tried to call him, but his phone rang with no answer. She tried again. This time, her call was disconnected. She felt her body grow hot as she scoured over the text message again. This was not the Tyler she had known. The Tyler she knew loved her and wanted to marry her one day. He never made her cry, and he would never hurt her like this. She knew him. Emily felt a lump in her throat. Or did she? She had known the Tyler pre-accident. Post-accident-Tyler was someone else.

The backlight on her phone dimmed, blackening out the message. Emily wiped her sweaty palms on her jeans and looked around the room. The girl sitting next to her was marking some notes on her notepad in a neon color.

Emily cleared her throat, saying, "Excuse me..."

The student looked up at her.

Emily continued by asking, "Could I please use your phone for just a second to make a call?" Her voice was shaking, and the student looked concerned. Emily tried to explain. "My battery is dying." The lie came quickly. She just wanted to use another number to try Tyler on again. The student smiled and passed her phone to Emily. Emily promptly punched in his cell number and hit call.

The phone rang continuously but still, no answer. Emily bit her lip. She ended the call and handed the phone back to the girl, thanking her. He was not taking any chances with random calls. His message was loud and clear, and he had meant it.

Emily wanted to scream or burst into tears, but she couldn't do either in the middle of the library. She would wait to get home to fall into her mother's arms and let it all out.

Tyler had betrayed her heart and had discarded her like she was a useless rag. In the hospital, she had feared losing him. It had not crossed her mind that she could lose him after that too.

She thought back to the moment when he had held her in his arms at the airport. The difference in his embrace had been evident, but she hadn't wanted to read too deeply into it. But her instincts had been right.

Tyler had left her long before he had stepped on that plane.

Fifteen

Emily tried her best to concentrate on what Ian was saying. They had been on a video call for thirty minutes, and still, she couldn't pinpoint what the conversation was—something about honeymoon destinations.

It was difficult to rid her heart of the moment she and Tyler had shared the night before outside the church. The touch of Tyler's hands on her face still tingled on her skin. She hadn't expected to lose her emotions and bare her heart to him. But she had caved the moment he had apologized.

His apology reminded her of every possibility that could have been if he had not abandoned her; and the verbal avalanche overtook her good sense.

"The travel agent said we can make the payment next week, that is if your heart is still set on Tahiti." Ian's voice trailed off, and Emily chewed on the end of her pen, curled up on her bed.

In all the years, she had not considered the possibility that

Tyler had not intended to hurt her. He was dealing with his own grief and was so lost. She had seen that much in his eyes.

"Emily?" Ian's voice sounded irritated.

Emily dropped the pen from her mouth and repositioned her laptop screen. "Ian, I'm sorry. My mind went blank."

She saw him run his fingers through his hair as he let out a heavy sigh. "Em, I've heard that from you twice this week." He leaned back in his chair and crossed his arms. Emily knew she was in the wrong, but what was she meant to say to him? *Hey Ian, I can't stop thinking about my ex-boyfriend from twelve years ago, but sure, let's book the honeymoon tickets?*

Emily felt the frustration curdle within her. "Ian, it's been a tough week for me. I said I'm sorry." She let her head fall into her hands, and she heard the gentleness return in his voice as if he wanted to reach through the screen and hold her.

"Baby, maybe if you shared whats eating you, I would be able to help you. It can't be worse than being left in the dark like you're doing to me." He motioned at the travel brochures in his hand. "Or, worse than planning a honeymoon on your own, which I feel like I'm doing." He let out a soft laugh, trying to keep the conversation light-hearted. "And I'm terrible at the wedding planning stuff."

His eyes pleaded with her, but Emily knew that even if she were given a lifetime, she wouldn't be able to explain what Tyler's return home meant to her. Sooner or later, he would pack up and leave again, and she would have hurt Ian for no reason and fractured their future.

Candice may have been right; closure was probably what Emily truly needed from Tyler. He had apologized the night before. What else did she want?

Emily lifted her head from her hands and smiled ruefully at Ian. "You are right."

His eyes lit up. "About what exactly?"

Emily let out a single laugh. "You are bad at the wedding planning part."

Ian grinned and leaned back, locking his fingers behind his neck. "I may be bad at the wedding planning, but I'm going to be great at the marriage part." He winked at her, and Emily felt her anxieties from the night before diminish. Ian was what she needed; someone who knew what he wanted and wasn't afraid to forge through the messy stuff with her.

She picked up the pen again. "So, would you hate me if I changed my mind from an island destination to somewhere historical?" A change of subject is precisely what they needed.

The humor was back in Ian's face, and he leaned closer to the camera, his eyes soaking her in as he said, "Nothing in this world could make me hate you, Em." His voice was light again. "I can't wait to get home and see you. Maybe we just need a weekend of fun. All these business meetings and wedding plans are bound to drive anyone crazy."

Emily smiled at him, thankful for having someone like him in her life. They said their goodbyes and I love you's over the video before Emily disconnected.

She got off the bed and walked to her window. It was a beautifully clear Saturday. Before she could catch herself, she started wondering what Tyler was doing. She wondered how he was coping since their moment beneath the stars. Surely, he had some feelings to work through?

The butterflies tickled her middle area as the memory from the night before of his face inches away from hers returned. At the time, she had thought he might lose all resolve and kiss her. She hated herself for thinking that when she had a ring on her finger, symbolizing her promise to Ian. But she couldn't help it. The lines over the last few days had begun to blur over, making it impossible for her to see and feel what was right or wrong. She already felt as if she were betraying Ian for even giving Tyler any space in her mind.

All Emily knew was that when Tyler had left her twelve years ago, her heart barely found its rhythm back to normalcy. If he had leave suddenly again, she might never recover from it if she didn't get the closure she needed.

It's probably best if I'm the one who cuts us loose this time, she thought. In that way, the incomplete script of their lives could find its ending.

And, it would hurt less than if he had to break her heart a second time.

Tyler increased the volume on his phone as he took an afternoon jog through the neighborhood he had once been so familiar with. Most people would listen to their favorite playlist, but he preferred a selection of relaxing sounds of nature as his blood pumped through his body. His mind had been his worst enemy from the night before, prompting him to think about things he didn't want to.

The sun felt soothing on the back of his neck, and he soaked up its warmth as the sound of rushing streams echoed through his EarPods. He made his way around the familiar neighborhoods, darting in and out of streets.

Flashes of Emily's face appeared before him as he ran. He wiped at the sweat on his brow, trying to concentrate on the pavement in front of him. In one moment of having her so close to him, he had wanted to give in and stay that way forever.

Tyler wished he could rewind life; to get into a time machine and go back twelve years to have said anything else to her except goodbye.

Somewhere in his ocean of troubles, he had lost his way and his mind. How had he ever been so foolish to have let her go without a fight? So what if they didn't share the same faith and principles any longer? She was still the only one he needed in his life.

But now, he had to continuously remind himself that she was set to be married in a few months. The thought of knowing that another man was going to spend his life with the only woman he had ever loved made him want to hurl. He replayed her voice and words to him from the night before. She had needed him, and he had left her. She had even come looking for him to tell him that she would wait for him. And instead of being available to start over with her, he had been canoodling with whoever it was in college that day.

Tyler stopped running and leaned forward, his hands on his upper leg. He breathed heavily on the sidewalk. He wondered if given a choice if she would choose him now- after everything that had happened. If that was a possibility, she could move to his city and they could try to start over again, away from everything. Couldn't they?

His mind was a mess ever since he had been thrust back into his past. He shook his head, frustrated at the spiraling thoughts and possible scenarios taunting his heart.

He kneaded the base of his neck and took a look around. His surroundings suddenly seemed strangely familiar. Without realizing it, he had run right onto his grandfather's street. Tyler wiped at his forehead and looked at his grandfather's house in the distance. He wondered again what his parents planned on doing with the property.

He crossed the street with a light jog and made his way towards the house. An elderly couple was sitting on their porch chairs inside their yard as Tyler passed by them. They looked at him suspiciously. He raised his hand in a wave, but the couple ignored him. A part of Tyler wondered whether they had recognized him as Bill's grandson and chose not to greet him. He dismissed the paranoia.

He got to the front of his grandfather's house and hopped the short gate in one swift motion. He slowly made his way up the driveway, drinking the place in. He noticed the bird feeder was empty, and a sadness came over him. His grandfather had always made sure it was filled with seeds so that the birds could keep him company. He had always relished their chirping through the day.

Tyler could hear the trickling of the garden stream in the backyard, and he followed the sound of it around the house. A light breeze surrounded him, and he took in the crisp air, feeling refreshed after his run. The dew on the blades of grass flicked onto his legs as he walked through the path. The blades of grass were longer than usual, lacking the frequent maintenance his grandfather always attended to.

Tyler bent down and picked up a stone from the grassy embankment near the little stream. He ran his fingers over its smooth and wet edges, swallowing the lump in his throat. Something in him ached. His grandfather's words from that day on the porch echoed in him.

"There is no place in this world that is better than a home."

He sighed. *Home. Could I ever have that?* Tyler questioned.

Whilst in the midst of his musings, a car door shut behind him. Tyler frowned, dropping the stone to the ground, as he quickly made his way around the house to see if someone had come in behind him. His mother's Ford became visible, and he watched her round the corner nervously.

Her eyes met his, a look of surprise and relief washing over her at the same time. "Oh, so you are the intruder." She let out a single laugh and planted her hands on her hips. She had her cellphone in one hand.

Tyler felt sheepish but made his way towards her. "Whose

responsible for busting me? Are there cameras installed on the property that I'm not aware of?"

His mother chuckled, shaking her head. "Mrs. Stanley from down the road." Amusement was written all over her face. "She called me to say that a strange young man had just hopped Bill's fence." She took a breath. "I had a feeling it would be you. I was one road away, so I thought I would stop by. Just in case."

Tyler dusted his hands and found a spot on the porch stairs to sit down. He tried to explain. "I was jogging and somehow found myself here."

He saw something flash across his mother's face. A look of hope, almost. She smiled and came forward, perching herself on the edge of the porch steps where she had a clear view of him.

"How was the youth service last night? You came in after we had gone to bed and you left this morning before we could wake up." She didn't wait for him to answer. "Emily is doing a great job with those kids, don't you think?"

Tyler couldn't agree more. He fiddled with his EarPods in his hands. A question wrestled inside of him until he couldn't suppress it any longer.

"Mom, can I ask you something?" Tyler didn't know if he should open the book to the past, but the events from the night before were too overwhelming for him to keep it to himself. His mother was a good listener whenever he gave her a chance to be.

She frowned, concerned. "Sure, you can ask me anything." She leaned forward, never breaking eye contact.

Tyler took a breath. "Did you and Dad know that Emily came

to meet me a year after I had left home?" His question caught her off guard, clearly answering him.

"No, we didn't know," she said with a frown on her face. "Did you both get to talking back then when she did?"

Tyler let his gaze drop, replying, "No, we didn't. I may have been with someone else at the time when she came. She left before I saw her." He didn't want to divulge too much further on that subject.

His mother's face looked pained as she said, "That explains a lot." She leaned back against the stair railings and folded her hands in front of her. "Emily was very different after that first year had passed."

"Different, how?"

"She never asked about you again. She forged ahead with her life, worked a few jobs, saved, opened the coffee shop, ran with the youth group, and then Ian came along."

Tyler ran his hand through his hair and inhaled. "She thought I blamed her for that night, Mom. She assumed that was the reason I ended things with her."

His mother's eyes softened. She cleared her throat. "Well, that's understandable, Son. We all felt to blame on some level." She let out a sad sound, her eyes glowing with emotion. "In fact, we still do."

Her smile was kind, but Tyler felt the heat pulsate through his body. He propped his elbows on his raised knees and found a spot on the ground to stare at.

"I wanted to tell her so many things, but I just couldn't bring myself to do it. I also can't be selfish and ruin whatever life she's trying to build for herself just for the sake of getting some things off my chest, you know?" He paused and looked at his mother sadly. "I also didn't mean for any of you to feel as if I was angry with you all when I left. It had nothing to do with any of you."

His mother seized the opportunity to strike whilst the iron was hot.

"Son, how is anyone to know what you feel if you don't talk about it?" She shrugged, her voice pointed. "You don't include anyone's feelings in the decisions you make." She took a breath, sounding frustrated. "You gave Emily no choice but to move on. You gave your father and I no choice but to accept that you weren't coming home. We all tried to make the best out of a heartbreaking situation. Emily had her parents. Your Dad and I had each other. We also had your grandad." She sighed and fixed her gaze on him, asking, "What and who did you have in all these years?"

Tyler felt a sting in his throat at his mother's words. She certainly hadn't wasted time in laying it on him. When she put it like that, he was able to see how selfish he had been to all of them.

His voice dropped. "I had questions, Mom." He inhaled slowly. "Many, many unanswered questions. Even thinking about them makes me tired. I can't explain to anyone what I don't understand myself."

It was true. Every day he had new questions that added to the multiple he already had archived in his mind. And he couldn't find a way to talk through it.

His mother pursed her lips and put her hand on his leg. "Well, you aren't going to like what I have to say to that, but I'm going to say it anyway."

Tyler remained silent, surprisingly open to hear her perspective on it.

"Every answer is in the Lord, Tyler. It's found in His Word." She paused. "And that's why you haven't found the answers to your questions. You've been looking in all the wrong places for so long."

Tyler felt the weight on his shoulders grow heavy. Gabe, the grave-keeper, had said something similar- something about his focus being on the flood rather than on the rainbow. Tyler looked out at the road ahead. Had he really been looking in the wrong places? Had his focus really been on the glass half-empty this whole time?

A couple was strolling hand in hand while another man walked his retriever on the pathway. Tyler let out an exasperated sigh, and could hear the stubbornness in his voice fighting him.

"It still won't change the past, Mom." His eyes locked on his mother's, hoping she would understand his feelings. He expected her to oppose him and tell him that he was wrong. Instead, she squeezed his hand.

"Noah would want you to let it all go."

Tyler felt the air leave his lungs. Tears stung his eyes at the mention of Noah, and he gritted his teeth to keep them from rolling down. He didn't want to talk about Noah. He kept his voice even, saying, "Noah's not here, Mom. So, nobody can speak for him about what he would want."

"Yes, I can." His mother's voice was hard, and she stared at him, tears flooding her eyes. "I can speak for him because he was my son, and I knew his heart." Her voice softened as she touched his hand saying, "In the same way that you are my son, and I know your heart too. The only thing standing in your way to a happy and fulfilled life is you, Tyler."

The knot in his throat grew tighter and he struggled to swallow. The pain in his mother's eyes was unbearable to look at. How could he explain that he felt guilty for even thinking about a future of his own when he had robbed his own brother of his? How could he ever be happy knowing that? How could he build his life on the death of his brother?

His mother wiped at a tear and let her hands drop with a smack on her legs. "And you are right about one thing, Tyler." She kept her voice low as she stood up to leave. Her eyes remained fixed on his.

Tyler waited for her to continue.

When she did, he felt as if a needle pricked his heart.

"Nothing can change the past, Son. But you can change your future."

Sixteen

Michael did not want to burst his wife's bubble as she relayed the conversation that had transpired the day before with Tyler. Even as they drove to church, Beth's tone was filled with excitement- the kind Michael had not heard in her voice for many years.

"I felt as if it was a true breakthrough, Mike. It was the first time we made progress with such a discussion." She turned the radio volume down and angled herself towards him as he drove. "I don't know what happened between Emily and him at the youth meeting, but something happened that has him questioning a lot. I saw it in his eyes, Mike. He is too proud to delve deeper into his issues, but he was yearning for answers." She lifted her hands while saying, "Maybe Emily is causing him to feel things again and wonder about his future. Maybe that's going to change something in him. If she feels the same way, what if that makes him stay?"

A soft sigh escaped Michael's lips as he stayed focused on the road in front of him. When he didn't respond, Beth slumped back in her seat, and her tone fell flat.

"You don't think that's possible? You think I'm reading too much into it? Am I clutching at straws?"

Michael looked at her, surprised, before taking her hand assuredly. He kept his eyes forward on the road ahead. "That's not it at all, Love. I don't dispute the feelings between Tyler and Emily. But, what I do know, is that Emily cannot save him from what he's running from. And it would be unfair to her if he weighed her down with his double-mindedness. If he returns home, it shouldn't be for Emily."

He felt his wife's hand loosen in his, as she let out a breath. She blew at a wisp of hair and stared outside the car window. He felt horrible at how her tone suddenly dropped to sadness again. "You're right. I guess I just saw some flicker of hope."

"And a flicker of hope it was, Beth," Michael stressed his words. "I'm only saying that realizing what Emily means to him is not even half the battle here. Even if they ride off into the sunset together, our son would still be fumbling in the darkness of his past." He tightened his grip on the wheel. "His soul is on thin ice. Only the Lord can heal him."

They turned into the church driveway and headed towards their designated parking space. Families waved at their arrival and a few of the youth smiled at them.

Michael watched them pass and let out a groan as he spoke."-Tyler could be greatly used by God if he would just surrender. What he went through as a teenager can be channelled into such purpose. He can reach so many people whom others can't." He unfastened his seatbelt and turned to his wife.

Her shoulders dropped as she nodded, saying, "I agree, Mike. I am hoping for that too."

Michael smiled. "And those who hope in the Lord are never disappointed, Beth." He leaned forward and kissed her cheek before adding, "So, let's do what we do best. Keep hoping."

The tide of his heart had started to turn, and Tyler didn't like it. He struggled that entire Sunday morning as his parents were preparing for the church service. It brought back a tsunami of memories of the good old Sundays when all four of them would be rushing about, trying to wolf down breakfast, and scramble to the car while his father would be hooting and waving them in.

The thought had crossed his mind to get dressed and join them, even if it meant sitting stone-faced in the back of the church. Something about his mother's words the day before, about him looking for answers in the wrong places, had resonated with him on some level. But he just couldn't bring himself to go. He didn't want to fall prey to his conflicting emotions, and he didn't want to give anyone false hope with his presence at the church either. Being inside the church on the day of the funeral and at the youth meeting had been more than enough.

Tyler had expected them to invite him to the Sunday morning service, and he wasn't looking forward to turning them down.

But, surprisingly, they had not asked him to. Instead, they quietly left through the front door. From Noah's bedroom window, Tyler had watched his father open the car door for his mother. They reversed out the driveway and disappeared down the road.

His mother's words rang in his ears again.

"Every answer is in the Lord, Tyler."

Tyler couldn't help but wonder if that was true. Emily and his parents had faced a similar loss and guilt when Noah had died. Yet, because of their faith, they had been able to move forward. He was the only one hanging in limbo, uncertain about what he was truly running from, and unsure about where he was going with his life.

Tyler's thoughts were interrupted as Candice placed the plate of pancakes in front of him, asking humorously, "She told you to get the pancakes, didn't she?"

Tyler let out a single laugh at her question as he reached for the golden syrup to drizzle over them. "Candice, Emily used me as her pancake-guinea pig for years. I may as well see if my tips and criticism has paid off."

Candice let out a chuckle and wiped her hands on her apron, waiting for him to take his first bite and hand down the judgment. He swallowed a forkful and rolled his eyes back deliberately.

Candice laughed out loud. "I'm guessing by that reaction, it means it paid off."

Tyler grinned and took a sip of his orange juice. There was a look of hesitancy on her face before she asked, "So, you weren't in the mood for church today?" She kept her voice conversational while looking around the coffee shop. "The café usually gets busy in the next half an hour once congregants start strolling in for their lunch after the service."

Tyler wanted to correct her. He hadn't been in the mood for church for twelve years. Although he had felt a bit differently that morning, he didn't want to get into it with her.

He wiped his mouth after taking another bite and shrugged. "I guess you could say I'm what they call a backslider."

He noticed the compassionate look fall across her face. Her tone was kind, but her words hit him unexpectedly as she said, "There's no such thing as a backslider." She cocked her head to the side. "Because those who truly know the Lord can never leave Him in the first place."

Tyler felt the forkful of pancakes get lodged in his throat. He reached for his orange juice and gulped some of it to swallow the lump down. Tyler knew Candice wasn't trying to be rude or inquisitive. He quite enjoyed her friendliness, but he wasn't expecting her to be that direct with him. He wondered what Emily had shared with her. Her eyes seemed to know more about him than he thought she did.

Candice lowered her head, looking slightly uncomfortable at her candidness. She motioned at his food, speaking politely. "Enjoy your brunch. Shout if you need anything."

He watched her go back to serving another table and pondered her statement. Was it true? Had it been easy for him to walk away from his faith because he never really had it in the first place? And just when Noah had helped him make sense of a lot of the questions he once had, the accident had happened.

Tyler put his fork down and pushed his plate to the side, suddenly losing his appetite. The question swirled in his mind just as the front door opened, and a familiar woman walked in.

Tyler knew he had seen the woman from somewhere before. Her blonde lengths hung around her elbows, and she had on a cherry-red shade of lipstick applied. Her eyes suddenly fell on his, and a knowing look crossed her face as if she recognized him. Tyler couldn't help but look over his shoulder, wondering if she was looking at someone behind him instead. When he looked back at her, she flashed him a pearly white smile and lifted her hand in an apprehensive wave.

Tyler forced a smile in return and shifted uncomfortably in his seat, turning his attention back to the half-eaten pancakes on his plate. He lifted his eyes slightly and watched Candice ring up the woman's order at the counter. The woman looked over her shoulder at him again, her eyes glued to him. Tyler cleared his throat and broke the eye contact. She started sauntering towards his table, wearing a tight-fitting knee-length skirt and a white blouse tucked in neatly.

Tyler noticed two other men look up from their newspapers and coffees when she approached his table. She was attractive, no doubt, in a sort of look-at-me way.

Her voice was flirtatious when she reached him. "5F!" She grinned, amused at herself.

Tyler frowned but kept a polite smile on his face. "Excuse me?"

"5F. That was your seat."

Immediately, Tyler remembered. She was the air hostess from his flight a few days ago. He let out a single laugh. "Oh, yes. Hi…"

She put her hand out, her nails manicured in bright pink. "Hi, I'm Terri. And you are?"

Tyler fought the urge to say *not interested*, but he didn't want to come off rude. He also didn't want Emily to walk into her coffee shop and think he was chatting up some strange woman. It wouldn't be the first woman she would have seen him with. That thought alone brought back a pang of guilt in him. He kept his tone polite, shaking the woman's hand.

"I'm Tyler. It's nice to meet you, Terri."

"So do you live here, Tyler, or are you on business?" Her grey eyes batted at him.

Tyler cleared his throat. "Uh, I'm just visiting." An awkward silence followed, but her eyes were still fixed on him, inviting him to keep up the conversation. He returned the question. "And you?"

She threw her hair over her shoulder and did something he wasn't expecting. She pulled the chair out from across from him and sat down. She explained that she was in town from the night before and was flying out again in the morning. Tyler shifted in his seat, uncertain as to what had just happened. It wasn't that he was timid around women. Over the years, Tyler had become quite a master at this sort of interaction. Many times, he had pursued it first. But something in him felt uneasy in light of all that had transpired over the last few days since he was back.

Watch and pray, that ye enter not into temptation: the spirit is indeed willing, but the flesh is weak.

Tyler felt as if an electric current coursed through his body. It was the same verse that had flashed on his phone the day of the accident. Tyler felt his throat close, and he reached for the last bit of his juice.

Just then, Candice walked over to their table with Terri's coffee in her hand. Her eyes held confusion as it slid between the two of them, probably itching to know how Tyler knew Terri.

Tyler pushed the glass aside and spoke to Candice quickly. "Can I pay and get these to go?" He pointed at the leftover pancakes.

Terri looked disappointed as Candice removed the plate from the table. As Candice turned to leave, Terri spoke in a sultry tone. "So Tyler, I'm staying at The Vintage Inn, which is a few roads from here."

Tyler knew the place well.

Terri continued. "There's a great little bar on the outside that I heard is a must. If you're free later tonight, then maybe we could meet for a drink?"

There it was. Tyler remembered how quickly he would have taken a woman up on that offer a few days ago. But he couldn't shake the verse that had come to his mind, or the sudden unfamiliar discomfort he felt under a flirtatious woman's advances.

He kept his tone even. "I'm sorry, Terri, I won't be able to join you. But you have a safe flight back home."

Her eyes stayed fixed on him as he rose from his chair and

walked to the counter where Candice was preparing his take-away.

Candice shared a subtle smirk with him as he took his wallet out, her voice sarcastic. "I'm guessing that was not a long lost cousin of yours from the neighborhood?" She wrinkled her nose at him. "I can't see the resemblance."

Tyler couldn't help but let out a chuckle. He still felt taken back by the verse that had come to him. He didn't want to overthink it. But, the last time when that had happened, and he had disregarded the warning, tragedy had struck. He didn't want to chance it this time either. At least not while he was back in town.

"That's not a cousin, Candice. It's one of Tyler's fans." Emily's ridiculing voice caused Tyler to jump, as if he were caught red-handed in the act of something illicit. He turned and saw her round the counter. He hadn't seen her come in, but she had obviously observed enough to make such a comment.

She was dressed in a simple emerald-colored dress, just below the knee, with a black beaded design around the collar area. The color of the dress only made her green eyes stand out more than usual. She had little heels on and a simple gold watch across her wrist. Even in her simplicity with minimal makeup on, Tyler caught his breath at the sight of her.

Candice let out a laugh and nudged Emily playfully. "Give him a break, Em. She approached him. I witnessed the whole thing. He's even taking his pancakes to go!"

Emily rolled her eyes and grabbed an apron from under the counter, tying it around her slim-waist in one quick motion.

"Don't defend him, Candice. I'm not surprised. Tyler does have a thing for blondes." Her tone was taunting, and Tyler couldn't help but wonder if the sarcasm was her way of hiding her jealousy. A part of him relished it. He shared a knowing look with Candice, who also seemed to pick up on Emily's tone.

He decided to have fun with her as he leaned forward, saying, "Emmy, the last time I checked, so do you."

Her face flushed red, and Candice roared with laughter. Tyler chuckled with Candice and kept his tone light and teasing as he winked at Emily. "But you can rest peacefully knowing you were, and always will be, the only brunette in my life."

Emily glared at them both, trying to keep a straight face, although Tyler saw the hint of a smile break free.

Emily hated the effect that Tyler had on her. His personality was a magnetic force that she couldn't avoid. She didn't consider herself a weak woman, except when she was under his gaze. Even in the most uncomfortable situations, he somehow found a way to make her fold and give in to his charm and wit.

She had been parked outside, the phone to her ear, when she had seen Tyler sitting inside the coffee shop. He had been absent from church that morning, but she wasn't expecting to see him at *Emmy's* either.

The sight of him caused her heart to stir. Emily watched as a tall blonde woman walked up to him, engaging him in a conversation. Emily's insides twisted as a wave of jealousy ripped through her when the woman sat down with him. Emily couldn't blame him. Tyler was an attractive man. *And single*, she had thought.

Now that she was behind the counter, facing him, her face felt flushed under his charming gaze. He was leaning forward, teasing her, while Candice laughed along with him. As much as Emily enjoyed the banter, her decision from the day before weighed heavily on her heart. She would have to make her intentions clear. She was marrying Ian, and the unfinished chapter of their lives at nineteen years old needed to come to an end. The thought of having that conversation made her edgy, but she composed herself enough to jot down some details on an invoice.

"Candice, I'm heading over to the park with these cupcake deliveries. Mrs. King is having her daughter's birthday party near the lake. About forty kids are waiting for their sugar rush today, and I don't want to keep them waiting."

Candice moved the pink boxes of cupcakes from the pastry counter to the front, blowing at a wisp of hair. "How are you going to carry these boxes by yourself?"

Emily looked at Tyler intentionally. "Romeo over here can put himself to good use."

Candice chuckled at Emily's jab. A humorous and surprising look crossed Tyler's face as he straightened, saying, "Sure, Emmy. I'm happy to help. Should I get these in your car so long?"

Emily handed him her keys, and they watched him grab the boxes and head for the door.

Candice flashed Emily a confused look, asking, "Am I missing something? You both spending time together now?"

Some customers walked past and greeted Emily. She waited until they were out of hearing range before glancing back at Candice. "We got caught up in a moment on Friday night."

Before she could continue, Candice's eyes grew wide as she interjected, "Emily… what happened?"

Emily let out a sigh. "Something that cannot happen again. It's just that everything came rushing back, and emotions were raw." She sighed. "Tyler and I need to start over by drawing some lines between us. He took himself out of the picture years ago. We can be friends." Emily tried to keep control of her voice.

Candice was about to say something in response when Tyler walked back in for the next set of cupcake boxes. He was about to head back out when the blonde woman got up from her seat, walked past him, and smiled alluringly. The woman's voice was teasing as she said bye to him. Emily watched Tyler smile politely back at the woman and return the goodbye. When he caught Emily staring at him, Emily broke her gaze from his and returned her attention to the invoices. She didn't want him to think she was jealous.

The moment he was out of sight again, Candice spoke, her eyebrows raised but with a snarky tone. "I wish I had a friend that looked at me the way you two still look at each other."

Emily rolled her eyes and looked out the window. She watched as Tyler packed the boxes into her car. Candice must have sensed her apprehension. She reached across the counter and took Emily's hand in hers.

Her voice was compassionate as she said, "Emily, make sure you know what you're doing." She smiled gently as she continued. "Sometimes the heart can't follow through with what the brain decides to do."

<h1 style="text-align:center">Seventeen</h1>

Tyler carried the last cupcake box to the party table where several little girls in white ballerina outfits and princess dresses sat. They giggled excitedly as he opened the lid of the box and their eyes fell on the treats inside. A few squeals were unleashed.

Emily was standing nearby, talking to the birthday girl's mother. Tyler still couldn't help the curling in his middle whenever he looked at her. Her brown hair swirled below her shoulders, and her laughter rang in his ears. He had been surprised that she had wanted him to accompany her on her business errand. He wasn't complaining. Any moment with Emily removed his mind from some of his burdens.

Around her, he was like a moth to a flame.

He dusted his hands on his jeans and waited for her to finish speaking with the lady. She caught his gaze, smiling at him from time to time. She said goodbye to her customer before quickly joining him at his side. Tyler angled himself towards the car, but she stopped him, her tone light.

"Tyler, do you want to walk with me for a bit?"

He did want to. He also couldn't help but recognize an urgency in her voice. He motioned towards a pathway that led around the lake. Many families were out on the grass, having picnics while their children played with frisbees or kicked a ball around with a dog in tow. It was the perfect Sunday afternoon picture- a picture he may have had with her had things been different. He was aware of how closely she walked beside him, and he was careful not to let their arms touch. Her eyes were on some of the children who were playing a few yards out. He watched her as she smiled at the kids.

A question fell out of his mouth. "You and Ian plan on having a family soon?"

She kept her eyes ahead and tucked her a few strands of her hair behind her ear. "Well, a family is always in the plan." Her tone was a little unnatural. She then looked over at him, asking, "And are you planning on meeting up with Miss Long Legs later on?"

For a moment, Tyler had no idea what she had meant until suddenly, it dawned upon him. He let out a laugh, running his hand through his hair. The air hostess at the café had really crept under her skin.

"You're still on that?" He raised his eyebrows at her. "But no, I'm not meeting with her later."

They were walking near the edge of the lake. The gentle swishing of the waters on the banks was serene. A few ducks paddled across to a group of children who were throwing bread crumbs at them.

Emily shrugged, her eyes fixed ahead. "Why not? Aren't you planning on finding someone and having a future with them? I thought by now you would have."

An odd sensation stirred in Tyler. Why was she suddenly interested in his love life? Was she trying to tell him something? Or, instead, was she trying to get a reaction out of him?

He cleared his throat and looked out at the lake. A boldness came over him. "Well, to be honest, nothing has ever come close to what you and I shared, Emmy. So, what would be the point?"

Her face fell, and he noticed she had slowed her steps. He shoved his hands in his pocket and slowed down so that he was still next to her. He tried to probe at her too. "I guess I haven't found what you seem to have with Ian."

He tried to notice if there was any reaction to his statement. But her face was blank. She crossed her arms and looked out at the lake, her brows furrowed. Her green eyes looked distant, deep in thought. Unexpectedly, she came to a complete halt, angling her body towards him. Tyler stopped, too, confused.

Her eyes searched his, and her expression was pensive. She worried her lower lip before speaking candidly. "If I asked you a question, would you be honest with me?"

A wave of nausea came upon him, and Tyler felt his heart rate quicken. Looking into her eyes made him want to tell her every truth inside of his heart. He tightened his hands in his pocket, bracing himself.

"I'll tell you whatever you want to know, Emmy."

For a brief second, it looked as if she had changed her mind. An anxiety fell across her face, as she struggled with forming the words. But suddenly, she surged ahead, asking, "If this is the last moment I'm ever in front of you…" She took a breath. "What would you say to me after all these years? Is there anything you would want to leave me with, before you go again?"

Tyler had never gone skydiving before. But, he had a feeling that the rush that swept over him may have felt something like if he had to jump out of a plane at ten thousand feet above the ground.

He wrestled with her question in his head. If he told her the truth, there would be no going back. It could change everything between them. It could even destroy the future she was planning with Ian.

Her eyes seemed to grow misty as she shrugged. "I know that question sounds strange. But, you didn't exactly leave me with much explanations twelve years ago. I guess before I move into this new season of my life, I would just like to have some kind of closure on the old one."

Tyler let out a deep breath. Her words struck him. She wanted closure. He searched her face. Did she want him to tell her that he was happy for her engagement, and that he wishes her well? Did she want him to tell her that they could be friends? Tyler felt the confusion slam around his brain. He couldn't say any of those things because it wasn't true.

And he didn't want to lie to her.

Tyler thought back to his mother's words. The past could not be changed but he could change his future.

Here goes, he thought.

"Emmy…" He watched the emotion creep into her face as he said her name. His tone was raw and meaningful as he allowed the words he had secretly harbored within him for years to escape his lips.

"I would say that I made the biggest mistake twelve years ago when I let you go. And if any part of you is willing to give me a chance, I would never make that mistake again."

Emily almost lost her balance. She was grateful for being out-doors because it felt as if the air was vacuumed out of her lungs in that moment. She needed to catch her breath again. For a moment, she wondered if she had imagined those words coming out of Tyler's mouth. She had waited for them for so many years that it was possible she made the whole thing up in her mind.

For twelve years, she believed that he didn't love her any-more, and that he had forgotten her for a different life. Now, he was standing in front of her, asking for a chance. She didn't know what she had expected him to say, but his answer was a shock to her system.

Emily felt her heart thumping. And with it came deep grief. Grief, for all they had lost and could have been if he hadn't taken twelve years to realize it. She didn't know how long she had been standing there, dumbstruck at the weight of his words. She stared at him, blindsided.

But after what felt like a lifetime, Tyler reached for her hand cautiously.

Don't do it, she urged herself.

She recalled what Candice had correctly said at the café earlier. Her heart was unable to follow through with what her brain had decided was the right thing to do. The right thing to do was to tell him that he was too late. The right thing to do was to wish him well for the future and head back to her plans with Ian. But she couldn't fight how right it felt whenever he looked at her, and whenever he said her name. Being with him took her back in time; all those days had his face in it.

She felt his fingers weave between hers, the brush of his skin stirring the butterflies within her. She did nothing to stop the moment. Everything in her desired him to keep going. The feel of his hand in hers caused a knot to form in her throat. She searched his eyes and saw his own desperation for an answer from her.

Slowly, as if he wanted to give her every opportunity to pull away from him, he closed the distance between them. His hands met the base of her neck, and his lips finally found hers. The kiss was light but filled with longing. It left her breathless, and reminded her of their yesterdays- days filled with innocence and hope. It reminded her of what she had been missing in her heart for twelve years.

He kept kissing her as his fingers brushed through the sides of her hair. Emily didn't even realize that tears were sliding down her cheeks until she tasted the saltiness of them on her lips, mingled with his. He pulled away, his eyes fixed on hers. For the first time in twelve years, Emily saw him as the Tyler she had known before the night that had changed everything. He was looking at her in a way that proved that his walls were gone.

Almost whispering, he said, "I told you once before, there are many things I may be unsure about, or don't believe in. But you have never been one of them." He paused, his eyes hanging onto hers. "I have always loved you. No amount of time or circumstances have changed that. And that's the truth, Emmy. I don't want closure." He took a breath, caressing her cheek. "I just want you. You're all I need in my life." His voice was thick with emotion. "I don't want to leave again without you." He studied her eyes intently before saying, "Leave with me…"

With every word he said, Emily felt an exhilarating rush. Her heart was racing where she was certain he could hear it.

But, suddenly, she felt something else.

As if the sound of an alarm bell pierced the beautiful dream she had become captivated in, Emily stared at him wide-eyed, a realization consuming her. His words caused the penny to drop in her heart.

What he was asking for, she couldn't give.

She felt her eyes grow large as she peeled herself away from his arms and breathed heavily, her voice trembling as she managed to say, "Tyler, I can't do this."

She felt ashamed at herself for wanting to ignore the warning bells and find his lips again. But she couldn't ignore his words nor the request that had slipped out his mouth.

Tyler's face looked hurt and confused by her reaction. He stepped forward, asking, "What do you mean?"

Emily gulped and stepped back, hoping the distance between them would clear her head and not make her run back to him. She fiddled with the ring on her finger, and another tear slid down her face. She couldn't think about Ian right now and what this meant for their future. She needed to deal with the looming heartbreak at hand, despite being guilty of crossing so many lines already.

Tyler had been honest with her. It was time for her to be honest with herself, too, no matter how much it was about to hurt. She knew it was now or never. She couldn't tip-toe around his issues any longer. She had waited twelve years to say many things to him and this was the only chance she knew she would get.

"Tyler, I can't spend my life with someone who doesn't even know who he is." She saw that her words pierced him to his core. He was staring at her as if he was trying to make sense of what she was saying.

Her voice fought to stay gentle. "You're not the same person you use to be. We are both so different from who we were at nineteen."

She may as well have struck him across his face. He looked bewildered at her words, not expecting to have heard that. His tone pleaded with her when he spoke. "Emmy, listen to me..." He let out a deep breath. "I love you. And from every moment that has happened between us since I've been back, I know you still feel the same way about me. So, what do you mean? Are you saying we mean nothing to each other?"

He came forward, but Emily put her hand up to stop him. He honored her request and stayed rooted in his place. Emily felt her lower lip tremble and she tried to fight back the tears, but she lost that battle.

A couple walked past them, looking at them suspiciously as if it were apparent they were in the midst of a disagreement.

Huge teardrops fell from her eyes, and splashed onto her cheeks, making their way towards her chin. She brushed the moisture away with the back of her hand and found his eyes.

"Of course we mean something to each other. Tyler, I have loved you for half my life. I loved you enough to even let you go when you wanted me to." Her voice cracked as she said, "But you don't love the same way. Love is not in your words, Tyler. It's in your actions."

It was at that moment that Emily noticed his face pale a shade lighter. She wasn't sure what it was about her words that rocked him, but it did. The forlorn expression across his face brought a sword to her heart.

She pushed on. "You speak of love now, after twelve years of silence." She let out a sigh. "Even if we are together, it will never be enough for you. Twelve years ago, you had all the love in the world, and one horrible accident made you throw us all away." She took a step forward. "You turned your back on everything you believed in. It was so easy for you. Now, you're asking me to leave my life behind and follow you, when you don't even know where you're going."

Her words might as well have slapped him off his feet. She watched his expression grow defensive at the mention of the accident. The walls were back up, and his tone was cold when he spoke.

"Emily, wait. You think leaving my home, and leaving *you* was easy for me?" His eyes looked horrified at her comment. "And, what does the accident have to do with this?" He waved his arm between them, asking again, "What does it have to do with a possible future between us?"

Emily let out a single but sad laugh. "The past has everything to do with where we are today." She came closer to him. "What future can we have when you cannot even face what happened? You're desperately searching for someone to save you. I can't do that for you. Your freedom is found in the life that you've left behind."

She heard her voice grow louder. "You are just too proud to admit that you belong here. Your purpose is here. Your home is here. Your family is here." She swiped at a tear on her face. "I'm here…"

The air between them felt intense. She saw that her words were sinking into him, but he was trying hard to fight it off. She closed the gap between them until she was back in front of him. His nearness made her want to forget her good sense and take him up on his offer. But, instead, she reached out and placed her hand on his chest. She could feel his racing heart through his shirt.

Her voice softened. "God is love, Tyler. If you could walk away from Him, the One who loves you the most, how can you ever say that you would never walk away from me again? How can you truly love someone else, when you have rejected the greatest love of all?"

His eyes grew misty as she spoke each word. He broke her gaze and moved her hand off his chest, his body becoming rigid beneath her touch. Emily felt broken.

She noticed a group of teenagers make their way down the grassy banks in the distance. The sight of them triggered something in her. She kept her voice calm, and asked, "Do you want to know one of the real reasons I took on the youth group at church?"

Tyler's eyes found hers again. His posture spoke of defeat.

Emily smiled at him through her tears. "It wasn't just in honor of Noah." She took a breath. "Every lost teenager is a chance at having one less Tyler in the dark." She heard her voice crack as she said, "I never want there to be another Tyler, or another Emily in this world ever again."

A stray tear rolled down his face and he wiped at it quickly. Emily wanted to envelop him in her arms. She could feel his struggle, and she wished he would just wave his white flag and surrender.

When he spoke, his voice held defeat. "So, what does this mean for us? If we don't share the same faith, then we can't be together?"

Emily remained silent as his eyes searched hers frantically, as if he could somehow make her change his mind with his question. His tone dropped with disbelief as he asked, "Can you honestly go off and marry another man and live your life without me?"

The thought alone made Emily want to cave. He closed the gap between them and cupped her face in his hands again. His eyes were focused, his voice desperate. "Emmy, how would you be able to live your life each day without the one person you love? Tell me, please, because I let you go once, and I don't know how I will do it again."

Emily wanted to say that she didn't know how she was going to do it either. She couldn't imagine how hard this next goodbye would be, and she didn't want to walk away from him.

Everything within her cried out to God to give her the strength at that moment to do the right thing. A familiar peace came over her, and she reached up and held his hands against her face. She saw his features soften under her touch.

"Tyler," she said, her voice rich with emotion. "Do you know what is worse than living each day of your life without the one you love?"

She took a mental picture of his face, uncertain if she would ever see him again. Her answer was going to be one that he was not expecting.

Her eyes lingered on his before she spoke.

"Living each day without the One who is Life itself."

Eighteen

yler slammed the door of the taxi cab with such force that the cab driver looked over his shoulder perplexed while asking, "Bad day, Sir?"

Tyler spat out the address and stared out the window as the park faded from his view. His frustration was back with a vengeance. Just when he had let his walls down, even the slightest bit, it had backfired in his face. Again, a significant decision came back to the question of faith and God. Tyler felt his ears ring from the humiliation.

Emily's every word pierced him like a thousand darts. He couldn't understand how loving her and wanting her in his life had anything to do with faith. But, the words that had made him reel was when she had said something very familiar to the last conversation he had with Noah. Emily said that love was not in words but, rather, in action. He thought back to Noah's exact words.

"*It's very easy to talk about love. Not many people know how to do it.*"

He leaned his head back and ran his hands through his hair, staring at the roof.

Of course I know what love is, he thought. It's because he loved them so much that he could not get over what he had done to them. He caught the driver looking at him through the rear-view mirror.

Tyler gulped back the emotion in his throat, wrestling the anger within him. He would never be able to rid himself of the memory of her in his arms, nor the touch of her lips on his. He didn't regret telling her that he still loved her. But he regretted that he was twelve years too late. In that one moment, with her in his arms, he felt the sting from life's events ease. It had just been him and his Emmy. That one moment was a glimpse of what the rest of their lives could have looked like if he had not broken everything to pieces. Even though she had turned him down, that one moment would have to get him through the rest of his life.

Is it really too late for me? Tyler thought, while staring out the car window. His mistakes and stubbornness created a disastrous snowball effect on the lives of so many people, including his own. Perhaps he needed a self-examination of his life and choices. His head swam from the hurt in his heart.

He thought about how Emily would go off and marry Ian, a man who was probably better than he was. A man who had the same rock-solid faith as she did. A man who would never be a fool to say goodbye to her. The thought alone made him clench his fists and squeeze his eyes shut.

Is there any hope for me? Tyler asked himself.

"*Come now, and let us reason together… though your sins be as scarlet, they shall be as white as snow…*"

Tyler's eyes flew open at the voice. He looked at the back of the driver's head and frowned, asking, "Did you say something?"

The driver looked at him through the rear-view mirror again, his brows furrowed. "Uh, no, Sir." He paused momentarily. "Are sure you're alright? You look like you need to see a doctor."

Tyler did feel sick. The motion of the car and the overwhelming heat within him made him feel as if he was about to pass out, or hurl in the backseat of the vehicle. The nausea reminded him of the last few moments before the accident had happened. Tyler felt as if he couldn't breathe. He took a deep breath and wiped his sweaty palms on his jeans.

Coming back here was the biggest mistake, he thought.

Emily's words came back to him like a flood. "*You turned your back on everything you believed in. It was so easy for you.*"

Tyler gritted his teeth. How dare she say that to him? As if he hadn't lived every day of the last twelve years in despair and brokenness from his actions.

He leaned his head back again. He had turned his back on everything because he couldn't face what he had done.

Why would God have wanted him alive instead of Noah? Why didn't anybody understand the battle raging within him?

A tightening in his chest made it hard for him to breathe. It felt like an anxiety attack. He pressed his fist against his chest and inhaled deeply, feeling the pressure release. He needed to get his mind off everything, and he knew what could give him some temporary relief. He had stayed away from it since arriving. But, now, he needed to focus on something other than what he had just lost.

He tapped the driver on his shoulder to get his attention, saying, "Change of address."

"Sure, where to Sir?" The driver slowed down, waiting on him.

Tyler paused momentarily. Was he really too late in reviewing every decision and lifestyle choice he had made?

A sneering voice penetrated his thoughts. It was a voice he had not heard before- it was different from the other one.

"You've lost everything. Your home. Your brother. Your purpose. Your Emmy. And God let it happen. There's no hope for you."

Tyler felt the muscles in his jaw flex. The voice was right. What good could come from his life now? God had not stopped Noah from being taken away. And God had not stopped Emily from walking away from him either.

The image Tyler had of a possible future with her would remain just that- an image.

He studied the driver before speaking. "Drop me off at The Vintage Inn Bar."

Emily slammed her bedroom door shut and leaned her back against it, sinking to the floor in agonizing sobs.

She didn't know how she had managed to drive back to her

apartment in one piece with pools of tears clouding her vision. She felt them roll down her face, and she let her head fall in her hands, her shoulders convulsing from her cries.

All these years, she had secretly waited to hear those words roll off his lips. She had so many questions and waited for so many answers. And now that she had answers, she was not satisfied because none of the answers led her to where she wanted to be—with Tyler.

Did God really bring him back, only for her to say goodbye again?

She had fought so hard to convince herself that they were better off as friends. But she had lost that battle the moment his words were out of his mouth.

Any ordinary woman would have been over the moon to hear what he had said. And what he had asked. They would have taken him up on his proposition instantly. But Emily couldn't do it.

She knew that Tyler loved her the best way he knew how, but she also knew that as long as he chose to live in condemnation and on the run from his faith, they could never have a real future.

At nineteen, she had been prepared to leave everything and follow him to the ends of the world. But she was no longer a teenage girl.

She would be unwise to take that chance, building a life on the sand with him.

Everything about her life revolved around her belief in Jesus and her purpose. Having a future with Tyler would mean overlooking his stubbornness, pride and opposition to the things of

God. Any hurdle in their life could cause him to leave again.

She couldn't live her life with someone who was unreliable and double-minded. She couldn't marry someone who believed that God was cruel and that there was nothing to be grateful for. She couldn't risk having a family with someone who would never be able to teach her children about God and His love.

She let her mind dance back to the moment Tyler had kissed her. As guilty as she felt for betraying Ian, she couldn't deny how perfectly she fitted in Tyler's embrace nor how certain she was about what he still meant to her. But no matter how right it had all felt, it was still wrong. She had betrayed Ian.

Emily wiped at her tears quickly as she pulled out her cellphone from her bag. She scrolled to create a new text message. She typed in Ian's name. Her fingers remained unwavering on the keypad as she typed, *Please come home… we need to talk.* She hit send and leaned her head against the door.

She had always taught the youth group to find the treasures in dark places. And right now, as heavy as the darkness weighed on her heart for what she was about to do, she knew what the right thing to do was.

She would not allow herself to ruin Ian's chances of finding someone who was wholly devoted and confident in wanting to spend their life with him. Ian deserved a woman who knew, without a doubt, that she would love only him for the rest of her life. Even though their faith and interests matched, Emily knew their hearts didn't.

She was not looking forward to Ian's reaction to her betrayal.

He once said that he could never hate her. Emily was not sure about that anymore. It was going to wound her to her core when she told him the truth about everything. He had once asked her whether he had anything to worry about now that Tyler had returned.

She had promised Ian that he didn't. She had been mistaken.

Emily dropped her head in her hands, feeling like the worst person on the planet. But, she also knew that as long as she continued to breathe, she would never love another man like she loved Tyler Hill. And she couldn't help that.

No matter how damaged or lost he was, and no matter how hopeless a future with him seemed, their time spent together that day made her realize one thing.

Over the years she had tried.

But her heart had never found its way past him.

Nineteen

The numbness had returned, relieving Tyler of the havoc his heart had experienced that afternoon.

He didn't know how many drinks he downed, but the severe warmth in his chest gave him an indication. He leaned forward at the bar counter and ran his finger in a circular motion around the top of the glass. Tonight would be his last night in town. He had just purchased his one-way ticket back to his old life; a life that often helped him forget all he had lost and left behind, even if it was for a moment or two.

And he couldn't wait to leave again.

The bartender wiped down a glass and flashed Tyler a curious look, asking, "Another one, Sir?"

Tyler leaned his chin on the open palm of his hand and shrugged, replying, "Why not?"

The man poured another drink and slid the glass of the golden liquid towards him. Tyler picked it up, staring inside the glass. He glanced at the bartender before saying, "You know my father always talks about the glass being half-full or half-empty…" He could hear the exhaustion in his own voice. He pressed on. "Pastor Mike is his name!" Tyler let out a single laugh at himself and shook his head.

The man smiled nervously and continued wiping the glass in his hand. "Your father is Pastor Mike? From *The Father's House?*"

Tyler lowered his eyes, swirling the liquid at the bottom of the glass. "Yeah, that's him!" He paused and sat upright, staring at the bartender. "And I bet you know who I am."

The man had an amused smile on his face, waiting for Tyler to finish. Tyler gulped the drink back and let out a sigh.

"I'm the son who unfortunately made it out of that car wreck twelve years ago." He leaned forward and motioned at his glass to be topped up.

The bartender kept his eyes fixed on him for a moment. "Hold up. You were the miracle survivor from that accident?"

Tyler let out a sarcastic grunt. "Miracle? You would call a killer a miracle?"

The bartender looked perplexed. His voice lowered as he asked, "Were you driving the truck?"

Tyler frowned. "No, I was in the car with my brother." He paused. "Noah, was his name."

"But the truck driver caused that accident. So, how were you to blame?"

Tyler leaned forward, his eyes were small and focused. "Because, if it weren't for me, my brother would still be alive. And if it weren't for me, I would still have Emily today. And if it weren't for me, my parents wouldn't have lost a son. And if it weren't for me, my grandfather wouldn't have died without having the chance to say goodbye to me." He pursed his lips and raised his eyebrows. "Should I go on?"

The bartender looked confused. He exhaled as he crossed his arms and asked, "Sir, how about I call you a cab instead?"

Tyler checked his watch. He could barely make out the time. "No, it's my last night in town anyways. Why ruin it?"

The bartender shrugged and refilled his glass while speaking. "You know man, I'm not much of a faith-filled person, but I do know that accidents happen, and if you're still alive, it's for a reason. You just have to find yours."

Tyler stared at the glass in his hand. What reason was he saved for?

His grandfather's words crept in him. *God always a special blessing and plan for the youngest one. In time you will find yours and understand that.*

Tyler sighed. Even if there had been a plan for his life, he had wasted too much time. He was about to push the glass aside and call it a night when he heard a familiar voice at the other end of the counter calling his name.

"Tyler Hill!"

Tyler's pulse quickened as he glanced across the room. It was Ricky. Tyler felt winded at that moment. Ricky hadn't changed a bit. He still adorned that annoying Cheshire-cat-grin on his face.

And a drink in his hand.

Ricky let out an exaggerated laugh, saying, "I cannot believe my eyes! After ten years to see you here, of all places!"

The bartender gave them both a warning look. Tyler gritted his teeth.

This is the last thing I need, he thought.

He drew the glass closer to him and took the last swig. He then stood up and pulled the cash from his wallet, laying it on the counter towards the bartender, ignoring Ricky's advances.

The bartender collected the money and nodded at Tyler. "I'll get you your change. The concierge can call you a cab. Don't drink and drive."

Tyler nodded at the bartender just as Ricky's laughter rang out again. Ricky moved from where he was sitting and walked closer to Tyler. Tyler felt his fingers start to curl into his palm in a clenched fist; the closer Ricky got to him.

"Tyler, that's deep! He told you not to drink and drive!"

Tyler took a breath as the blood rushed through his veins. The bartender returned with his change. Tyler put the notes back in his pocket and turned to leave just as Ricky's jeering tone stopped him in his tracks.

"Come on, man! We can have a drink for old time's sake?" Ricky hesitated before continuing. "Noah won't be coming around to ruin the fun this time."

Before Tyler even processed his next move, Ricky had flown across the line of tables and chairs, knocking them to the ground. The contents of drinks and table snacks scattered to the floor, leaving a few guests horrified while they made their way out of the danger zone. A few of the female guests squealed in shock.

Tyler's fist ached as he took a few steps forward and towered over Ricky's body. Blood dripped from Ricky's lip as he stared back at Tyler, his eyes like saucers, bewildered from the blow. Tyler hunkered down and grabbed a fist full of Ricky's collar, yanking his upper body in a sitting position. Some of the other men in the bar tried to step in and separate them, but none of them were a match for the strength and adrenaline that was coursing through Tyler's body.

His voice was seething when he directed his words at his old so-called friend. "You know, Ricky, for years I wondered whether I hated myself or you more." Tyler glared at Ricky and went on. "I may never know. But, let this be the last time my brother's name ever escapes your mouth." Tyler growled, "Do you understand?"

Ricky swallowed, clearly receiving the message loud and clear. Tyler flung him back down and turned to leave, steadying himself. He passed the disapproving glares and stunned faces as he made his way out of the bar into the lobby of the Inn. The throbbing in his fist increased, and he noticed the bruising around his knuckles start to form.

He was about to approach the concierge to call him a cab when a woman appeared and spoke to him.

"So, you decided to take me up on the offer after all?"

Tyler turned to see Terri. She was wearing a champagne-colored dress with strappy heels. Her favorite accessory must have been the cherry-colored lipstick, which she didn't ever seem to be without.

He eyed her casually as he looked towards the door, saying, "I was at the bar for a few drinks. I was just about to catch a cab home."

She pursed her lips and walked towards him, invitingly. "Well, that's one plan. Another would be to escort me to my room." She ran her hand down his arm. "You can't pretend you didn't want to bump into me. I basically extended the invite earlier when you were playing hard to get." She giggled and continued, saying, "We could raid the minibar, and you could tell me how you got that shiner on your fist." Her eyes sparkled at him.

Tyler's head was spinning from the events of that evening, and he felt a heaviness come over him. There was no way he could go back home to his parents in his condition.

He glanced across the concierge desk at the clock on the wall. He caught his breath. *01:18.*

Unbelievable, he thought. He almost laughed out loud mockingly. What was it about the clock striking that time during significant moments? If God wanted to play those games with him, Tyler knew he could play them too.

Terri followed his gaze to the clock and turned back to him again. She looked confused as she asked, "You've got somewhere else you should be at this time?"

Tyler considered her words. Did he? What else did he have going for him in his life? He glanced back at the clock and felt the war inside of him rage on.

With that, he took her hand. "No, I don't have anywhere else I need to be."

Twenty

ichael ended the phone call and took a deep breath. He
stared outside the window towards the front driveway.
He wished the news was untrue. He felt hopeless after receiving
that information.

He rubbed the base of his neck and closed his eyes. He didn't
want to worry Beth, but she would find out sooner or later. People gossiped in small towns, and many were familiar with their
family.

Beth walked in, fiddling with her hands in front of her. Her
voice was anxious when she asked, "Was that Tyler on the phone?"

Michael couldn't blame her. This was not the first time they
had received a call past midnight about their son's whereabouts.
It didn't matter that he was now thirty-one years old. It still felt
like the night when he was nineteen.

"No, it was Hank from The Vintage Inn. He's normally at
reception for the midnight to morning shift. He saw Tyler and

thought he should call and let us know what was going on…" He saw Beth swallow as she came forward.

"Let us know what? Is he okay?"

"Tyler was at the bar there. He had a lot to drink." He flashed her a disappointed glance and took a seat near the fireplace. He tried to dismiss the uncomfortable twisting in his stomach. He rubbed his temples as he explained, "He also got into a fight with someone. And now he's with a woman whose staying as a guest at the Inn for the night. I don't think he will be home tonight." His own words made him feel sick. He rubbed the bridge of his nose and watched the worry wash across Beth's features.

Michael let out a sigh. "Hank was concerned about his condition, given the history. He didn't know if he was doing the right thing to let us know. I told him I appreciated it."

Beth folded her arms and moved in almost slow motion to the couch before sitting down quietly. "He did the right thing by telling us. Or, I would have assumed the worse all night long." She touched her mouth with her hands. "Something must have pushed him over the edge again."

He's been over the edge for twelve years, Michael wanted to say. Instead, he glanced at his Bible on the side table and felt the heaviness settle on his heart. Every time they thought they were taking a step forward, something happened that pulled them ten steps back.

"Michael, what do we do? Surely there's something we can do or say?"

Michael didn't know how to relieve his wife of the sorrow in her heart. Her eyes filled with tears, and she looked helpless. It was as if they both knew what awaited them in the morning.

The day had come again when their son would leave home and not look back. Michael rose from his seat and went to his wife to sit next to her. He reached for her hand. Her eyes met his, and he wiped at the stray tear on her cheek.

"We do the only thing we can, Beth." He took a breath. "Let's pray together."

Tyler stood at the front door of the house, hesitant to enter. His head throbbed from the last few hours, and he was riddled with guilt for his behavior. He hadn't planned on drinking while he was back home, and the last thing he wanted to do was fall into his usual destructive patterns after everything Emily had said to him. But whenever guilt overwhelmed him, impulsive decisions followed. And Tyler found it hard to gain self-control.

He unlocked his phone and found the electronic boarding pass in his inbox. He double-checked the departure time. His flight would leave in a few hours. It gave him enough time to pack his belongings and tell his parents goodbye before heading to the airport.

Emily's face dropped in his heart, and Tyler felt the muscle in his jaw flex. He had told her at her coffee shop that he would say goodbye before he left town again. Once more, he would be breaking a promise to her.

He took a deep breath and tried to turn the key in the door, but it was already unlocked. He frowned, stepping in. The house was quiet. He swallowed the lump in his throat, silently making his way to the staircase to go upstairs. When he passed the doorway to the living room area, he was surprised to see his parents sitting inside.

His father's eyes instantly met his. Tyler had never seen that kind of sorrow on his father's face before, not even when Noah had died. His mother let out a sigh of relief. She had probably been worried sick about him. Both his parents looked exhausted. And not just from a lack of sleep. It was a look of years of emotional weariness. Tyler felt the guilt stir in him. He had caused them to worry. Again. A simple text or phone call would have given them a few hours of sleep, but once again, he was too consumed with his own feelings.

Emily may have been right- his love was selfish.

His father motioned to the empty seat in front of him for Tyler to take a seat. Tyler imagined that this was what family interventions looked like. He shoved his hands in his pocket and made his way into the room, feeling like a teenager in trouble. *That's actually where it all started,* he thought. Despite being a man now, there was still a lost teenager inside of him.

He prepared himself for the tongue-lashing that was twelve years in the making. He sat down next to his mother, looking between both of them. But no rebuke came.

Say something, he thought as he clenched his fists.

Instead, his father reached for the Bible, which was on the

side table, and he opened it. Tyler felt his brows knit together. A Bible study was not what he was expecting. His father flipped through the pages until he suddenly stopped at a particular spot. He cleared his throat, and his eyes found Tyler's.

Tyler held his breath as his father read from the passage.

"Luke fifteen verses four to seven says, '*What man of you, having an hundred sheep, if he lose one of them, doth not leave the ninety and nine in the wilderness, and go after that which is lost, until he find it? And when he hath found it, he layeth it on his shoulders, rejoicing. And when he cometh home, he calleth together his friends and neighbours, saying unto them, rejoice with me; for I have found my sheep which was lost. I say unto you, that likewise joy shall be in heaven over one sinner that repenteth, more than over ninety and nine just persons, which need no repentance.*'"

With every heavy word that his father read out aloud, Tyler felt a peculiar heat flow throw his body. He had never heard or read that story in the Bible before. Something about it took hold of his heart unexpectedly. He could almost recognize himself as the lost sheep in the passage.

Would a shepherd really leave ninety-nine others to pursue the one that was lost? How did one missing sheep matter in comparison to the many others? What did that one sheep have to give that the other ninety-nine couldn't?

Tyler shifted in his seat and glanced at both his parents. His father seemed overcome with emotion as he wiped at his eye and closed his Bible.

Something about the atmosphere was charged, moving Tyler

to feel vulnerable. It was unlike a moment he had ever felt before. Not even when he had been in church.

His heart was giving way. He opened his mouth to ask what this was all about, but his father raised his hand slightly, stopping Tyler from interrupting.

His father found his voice and spoke soothingly.

"Tyler, when you leave here today, your mother and I don't know whether you will ever return home again."

Tyler was taken back. How had they known that he had planned to leave?

His father paused, gathering his emotions. "But we wanted to leave you with this reminder from the Word of God. If you re-member nothing else from this trip back home, remember this." He clasped his hands in front of him and continued saying, "There is no place where you can run or hide where the Lord can't find you or reach you. So you can leave again, but you know that you can never be the same again after these last few days back home."

Tyler felt his throat tighten. He wanted his father to stop talk-ing because he couldn't take the truth of those words. Tyler had not expected his return home to have eroded certain walls within him. He couldn't control what he was feeling, and he couldn't suppress the desires that were coming alive again. That's why he needed to leave.

But, even after a night of sin, Tyler still felt the overwhelming love in his father's tone radiate towards him. It was a love he could never understand.

He heard his mother sniff next to him, but he didn't want

to look her way. Something flickered over his father's face as he reached towards the side table for an envelope that was on it. Tyler didn't know what the envelopes was, but his father held it in his hand for a moment, as if he was considering what to do with it.

He then looked up and found Tyler's eyes, saying, "This is a letter from your grandfather to you."

The air felt as if it had left the room. A part of Tyler wanted to reach out and rip the envelope open right then and there to read his grandfather's words. But he hesitated, fearing the contents. What if his grandfather expressed disappointment at his choices? What if his grandfather had been angry at him for abandoning the family? Tyler wondered whether he even wanted to open the envelope.

His mother kept her voice a bare whisper, interrupting his chain of thoughts. "We were waiting for the right time to give it to you. But maybe that time is now. You can read it whenever you are ready to."

Tyler gulped back the emotion, and his brows furrowed. He could hear his voice quiver. "Do you know what it's about?"

His mother and father exchanged a look, but she was the one who answered. "We haven't read the letter, Son. We believe that part is personal." They didn't say much else, and Tyler felt as if they were holding back more information than they were letting on. Tyler reached forward and took it from his father's hand, staring at it blankly. His grandfather had thought of him before dying. The lump in his throat grew thicker.

His father broke the silence that followed, leaning forward. "Before you leave today, there is something we want you to know." His father took a breath. "There is something that we never told you all these years because we didn't think we needed to say it. But maybe as your parents, we were wrong for not saying it. So today, we want you to allow us to say it. You need to hear it from us."

A fear gripped Tyler, and he felt sick. He had no clue what was coming. He glanced at his mother, and she reached out and held his hand in hers, her tears trickling down her face. He felt the emotion in his throat, and he braced himself for it. His series of mistakes and bad choices had left him an open target for any criticism or rebuke from his parents. Tyler didn't know if he could take another heartbreak after all that had happened, but he saw the urgency in their eyes for whatever it was that they wanted to share with him.

His father rose from the seat and walked towards the couch where Tyler was sitting. He then hunkered down in front of Tyler as if Tyler were a five-year-old. The gesture moved something in him. He couldn't remember the last time when they had been physically eye to eye like that before.

His father touched his shoulder as his eyes locked on Tyler's as he spoke slowly and deliberately. The words were something Tyler would never have expected.

"Son…you did not kill Noah."

A deafening silence hung in the air. Tyler took in each word as if he were slow in understanding the language his father was speaking. When each word started to penetrate him, he couldn't fight off the emotions any longer. The sound of Noah's name alone caused the ground to feel unstable. He tried to shrug his father's hand off his shoulder. He didn't want to go through with the rest of the conversation.

But his father's grip remained tightened. Unrelenting.

His father spoke again, his tone more firm, as if Tyler had not heard him right at first. "Did you hear me, Tyler? You did not kill your brother. You were not to blame for Noah's death."

Tyler couldn't stop the tears. He found his voice, pleading with his father.

"Dad, please don't…"

The tears were streaming down his face now, overwhelming him and blurring his vision. He couldn't continue with his plea. His throat closed up.

His father edged closer, his eyes filled with deep sorrow, ignoring Tyler's protests. "What happened was a horrible accident that could have happened anywhere to anyone. You did not take his life that night." His father's eyes were fixed on his, not wanting to blink and break the moment. He smiled at Tyler sadly.

"Yes, you have made many mistakes, Son. But you do not have to destroy yourself because of them. You surviving was not a mistake." He tightened his grip on Tyler's shoulder. "The Lord does not make mistakes."

Tyler felt the heat intensify as tears rolled down his face. He buried his face in the crook of his own arm.

His father's voice pressed on. "There are consequences for

our actions. But, Jesus laid His own life down in exchange for ours so that we may find His grace and be redeemed. If Noah had to make a choice again about leaving that night to find you and bring you back home safely, he would do it in a heartbeat." His father's voice sounded choked up. "He would do it in the same way we all would do it for one another. That's what love is. That's what love does. That's what Jesus did when He left His Kingdom to come to this world to save us, despite the death He knew He would face."

The words moved Tyler like an avalanche that was held back for twelve years. It consumed every part of him.

That's what love does, Tyler thought.

Everyone had been telling him that love was in actions and not in words. He had only spoken about love, but everyone around him had shown him what love was.

Before he knew it, he fell into his father's chest, gripping him tightly, tears rolling down his face. His father's arms were around him instantly like he often did when Tyler was a little boy.

Tyler felt his mother's arms come around them both. It was the first time they had such a moment together, mourning the loss of so much that had happened.

His father's shirt was soaked with Tyler's tears.

Tyler felt himself choke back the sobs as he let his words roll from his lips, saying, "I feel I'm not deserving after everything I've done." He took a breath. "I didn't know how to build a life on the death of Noah."

His father's arms held him tighter. His words were slower as he responded, saying, "Son, nobody is deserving. That's why it's called grace." He let out a sad sound. "And you cannot build your life on the death of Noah. But you can build your life on the death and resurrection of Jesus."

He pulled back and studied Tyler's face. "And for full grace, there must be full repentance. Because, although you were not to blame for Noah's death," His father held the sides of his face tighter as he continued, "You, and only you, will be to blame for destroying your own life after God gave you a second chance at it."

Twenty One

he weather had been dull and miserable that entire week. It complimented Tyler's mood since he had left his home-town again.

The events of that day with his parents were still raw in his mind. It had been a struggle leaving under those circumstances, and since being back, he didn't feel at ease. He was physically present but detached from everything around him. He couldn't dismiss the yearning inside of him to see his parents or Emily's face again.

Something in him had changed since his father's words on the living room floor that day. It was a new, and unfamiliar emotion. He wanted to take each day slowly, afraid to make any impulsive decision.

He stood at the glass window of his office, overlooking the busy city below him. The view from the top floor always brought feelings of exhilaration. His company was one of the most lucrative marketing cooperations around, and it was a dream position for anyone his age. But even as he stood and stared at the city around him, he realized something. All his career achievements, financial gains, and commendable awards hanging on the office walls felt meaningless in light of all that he had truly lost over the years.

His father's words still rang in his ears. *You, and only you, will be to blame for destroying your own life after God gave you a second chance at it.*

Tyler sighed. Was his father right? Had he been given a second chance at life but had chosen to blow it? Had God spared him for a reason that he had thrown away?

All through the years, Tyler had believed that his escape from the accident had been a mistake. His father had said that God doesn't make mistakes. Those words had penetrated his heart.

Tyler rubbed his forehead. So many questions plagued him since he had departed a week ago. Before returning for the funeral, he had many questions about his past. And now that he had left his hometown once again, he had many questions about his future.

He walked back towards his desk and opened the middle drawer. The white envelope was positioned neatly on the top of other financial reports. He had been carrying his grandfather's letter with him everywhere. He was uncertain when the right time was to open it. He was still nervous about the contents. It saddened him that his grandfather never got the chance to tell him any of it in person, regardless of what the words were. Tyler would have loved the opportunity to hear him speak again.

He sighed heavily, holding the envelope in his hands. He was about to peel the corner of it open when his assistant sauntered into his office with a portfolio in her hand. She gave him a flirtatious smile and handed it to him while speaking.

"Mr. Hill – the campaign budget."

He left the envelope aside and took the file from her hand, flipping the clear sleeve open, perusing the figures. He was impressed with the company's strides. He placed it on the desk and ran his finger over a few of the report findings while asking, "Is my meeting with the marketing team still scheduled for later?"

She checked the tablet in her hand, scrolling down. "Yes, it's still at three-thirty."

Tyler noticed how she glanced over her shoulder as if to make sure nobody was coming in before she spoke again. Her voice was a whisper, asking, "So, do you want to grab a drink after work? Or, I could come over?"

Tyler cleared his throat. He closed the file on his desk and flashed her a polite smile. "I'm sorry, Jen. I've got a lot to catch up on and get through now that I'm back."

Her face fell, and she bit at her lip. "Are you doing okay, though?" Her tone was sincere.

Tyler stood straighter, replying, "Yeah, I'm doing good."

She nodded, even though his answer did not convince her. "You seem different ever since you've been back. Some of the others have noticed too."

Her words didn't surprise him. He had turned down several drinks and socials from his colleagues that week. The truth was that he felt out of his shell since being back, but he knew he couldn't explain it to anyone.

He let out a single laugh. "I'm doing fine. It was just a rough trip."

She shrugged and clasped her hands together. "Well, the offer is open for that drink if you ever change your mind. We had fun last month." She flashed him a flirtatious smile and turned to leave.

Tyler watched her go before he found his spot at the floor-to-ceiling glass windows again. He leaned against it, watching the cars pass while pedestrians hustled and rushed about down below.

He thought about Emily. She was probably forging ahead with her wedding plans, finally free to move ahead with the life she had chosen. A secret chamber of his heart was happy for her. Despite the consuming jealousy, Tyler knew that she would be happy with Ian.

And ultimately, her happiness was all that he cared for.

Because, sometimes, love meant letting go.

The café had been busier than usual. Emily was thankful for that because it helped get her mind off everything that had happened over the past week.

Candice was running around serving tables and punching orders in, with a new trainee following behind her like a puppy dog.

The new girl was a college student wanting to make extra cash for her acting classes. Emily watched as the girl took down notes furiously as she stayed close to Candice on the floor.

An elderly couple walked in and waved at Emily, motioning to their usual spot near the windows. Emily gave them the go-ahead nod and looked over at the new girl. "Table five need menus!"

The new girl grabbed the menus off the counter and scurried off towards the couple. Candice found her spot near Emily, her voice light. "I'm sensing she's going to fit right in."

Emily crossed her arms, watching the young girl make chit chat with the smiling elderly couple. "Yes, she's sweet. Reminds me of when you first started."

Candice laughed and nudged Emily before walking off. "Yes, well, don't forget me, Emily."

The sound of those familiar words stirred Emily's heart. *"Don't forget me, Emmy…"*

She felt the lump in her throat at the reminder. How could she ever?

She made her way to her usual spot at the back of the café. It was hard glancing around the café and not remembering the moments when Tyler had been there, poking fun at her.

She wondered how he was doing. News had travelled fast about Tyler's activities the night before he had left. In a small town, people gossiped a lot. She had felt a sinking pit in her stomach when she had heard that he had spent the night with a woman before leaving. Emily didn't want to blame herself, but she did question whether she had been too harsh with him at the park. She also overheard that Tyler had, in no uncertain terms, put Ricky in his place. A part of her felt satisfied about that.

Twelve years ago, Tyler had broken her heart, and she had never healed from it. But seeing his face as she broke his was a different ballgame. He had given her a choice to choose him, and leave with him. And she had turned him down. She prayed that in time, he would understand why.

The front door opened, and she saw Beth walk in. The woman's eyes were downcast. Emily watched as Candice greeted Beth at the door, and they exchanged a few words before Candice pointed at Emily in the back. Emily raised her hand in a small wave as Beth made her way towards her.

Emily stood up and gave her a quick side hug. "It's nice to see you, Beth."

Beth squeezed her for a moment longer before sitting down. "How are you doing, Em? I was visiting a friend nearby and thought I would check on you. You've been quiet this week."

Emily sighed and lifted her shoulder casually, replying, "It's been a rough week."

Beth let out a single but sad laugh, and put her purse on the table. "It's been a rough decade for all of us."

A silence hung between them, and Emily noticed the moment when Beth glanced at Emily's left hand, a knowing look passing over her face.

Beth let out an exasperated sigh. "Oh, Emily! I'm so sorry. I didn't know."

Emily played with the space on her left hand and pursed her lips. "It's been hard, but I know I did the right thing."

Beth reached across the table and put her hand over Emily's. "How is Ian doing? I will tell Pastor Mike to reach out to him, but I don't know if he will take it in good spirit, given the sensitivity of the situation."

Emily tucked her hair behind her ear as Candice brought Beth her usual order- berry tea. She waited for Candice to leave before saying, "Ian has nothing against you or Pastor Mike. He just needs some time to heal." She paused, wanting to bare her heart to someone. "Do you know what he said to me when I called the engagement off?"

Beth put her tea down and waited patiently. Emily blinked back the tears, remembering the devastation on Ian's face. She may as well have driven a stake right through his heart when she had told him what had happened.

"He said he saw it coming."

Beth's eyes widened, a sympathetic look on her face. "Really? He actually said that?"

Emily leaned back and crossed her leg over her knee, nodding slowly, while saying, "He said that he felt it from the moment he saw my face at the funeral."

Beth stirred her tea and let out a sigh. "Sometimes, others can see things we can't."

"Or, that we choose not to." Emily responded. She folded her hands on the table before asking, "Have you heard from Tyler?"

A concerned look fell across Beth's face as she replied, "Surprisingly, he messaged his father a few days ago saying that he was thinking about us and that he loved us." She took a sip of her tea. "We are just praying God wrestles with him until he gives up this foolish fight." She pushed her drink back and shook her head. "You know, Emily, condemnation is such a cruel thing. It's a destiny killer. Nobody can understand it unless they have felt the weight of it on their shoulders. And Tyler has carried that with him for twelve years."

Emily felt tears in her eyes at Beth's words. Beth was right. Tyler's burden of condemnation had caused a ripple effect across all their lives. It had sucked away every dream and hope for the future. It had robbed them all of time and purpose.

Emily wondered whether she had given up on him too soon. Perhaps, she had cut him off because of the consuming betrayal she had felt.

Tyler's question from the day of the accident suddenly returned to her mind. *"That's what Jesus would want us to do? Cut people off because they are different than us?"*

Emily felt her stomach tighten. Had she done the right thing?

Beth leaned back, her eyes filled with compassion as she spoke. "So, we will continue hoping that God finishes what He started. I don't believe that Tyler opened his eyes in that hospital for nothing. Some sort of beauty will come from this brokenness. One day, he will be back where he belongs."

A smiled lifted the corners of her mouth before she asked Emily a question. "What do you plan on doing going forward?"

Emily knew the answer before she was asked. "I'm going to

do what I should have done twelve years ago, Beth." Emily looked outside the café windows, as she spoke quietly.

"I'm going to pray, and wait for that day too."

Twenty Two

Tyler knew instantly that he was dreaming.

There had never been a place more serene and radiant with light than where he stood. An unexplainable warmth surrounded him. He felt as if he were within a cloud.

In the distance, a shadowy figure started to make its way towards him. Tyler couldn't recognize the figure, yet he knew the person was familiar to him. As the figure drew closer, Tyler felt his breath catch in his throat. An overwhelming sensation took hold of him as the individual's face became clear.

He let out a trembling gasp, saying, "Noah?"

Noah stood before him, looking brilliant as ever. He was adorned in an off-white robe with an intricate golden design around its edges. Tyler had never seen such attire before. There was a look of wonder on Noah's face. Tyler couldn't put an age to Noah's being. He looked young and mature at the same time.

Noah's voice sounded like an echo when he spoke his name.

"Tyler…"

Tyler felt choked up at the sound of his name on his brother's lips. He took a step forward, puzzled. "I don't understand, Noah. Where are you?"

Noah continued smiling, even as he spoke. "I'm home." His eyes grew soft as they locked on Tyler's. "The real question is, where are you?"

The question stirred Tyler. He felt a heaviness inside of him. He kept his eyes fixed on Noah's. He didn't want to flinch or blink just in case he lost his brother and woke up from the dream.

Before he could think of an answer, his mouth opened, and the words fell out. "I'm lost, Noah," he took a step forward and said, "I felt as if I robbed you of your life that night. I wanted to say I'm sorry, but it was too late."

Noah's eyes flickered a shade that Tyler had never seen before. The smile never left his face as he spoke. "Our time is in the Lord's Hands, little brother. And there's no place I would rather be than where I am right now." Noah looked over his shoulder towards the place where he had appeared from. Tyler couldn't see anything through the distant white mist.

Noah let out a delighted sigh, saying, "If only you could see the place He's prepared for us."

The atmosphere around Tyler danced with sunlight rays and shimmering golden dust. He had never experienced such a joy before. He searched Noah's eyes and asked, "Noah, can't I stay here with you?"

A look of curiosity washed over Noah's radiant face. He tilted his head to the side. "Do you believe, Tyler?"

Tyler felt a lump get lodged in his throat. His voice was a whisper when he answered, saying, "I want to believe again," he glanced behind Noah and continued, "I think I'm starting to..."

"Then believe." Noah's voice was firm in its compassion. "Only those who believe will call this Home."

He reached out and touched Tyler's shoulder. Tyler felt the flood of tears pool his vision at the feel of his brother's hand on him. He was real! The sensation of his hand on Tyler's shoulder was more real than any moment in their lives before.

Noah spoke slowly this time. "You've allowed the enemy's voice to rob you of so much." He paused and let the words echo in Tyler's ears. "You spent years questioning where the Lord was. But He was always there. He never left you. You were the one who left. Time and time again, He has reached out to you."

The tears overwhelmed Tyler's vision. He blinked and felt them roll down his face. His brother brushed a tear off his face, kindness etched in his eyes. Noah's voice was tender as he asked, "Why do you choose to carry all this hurt on your shoulders, when He carried the cross for you?"

The words pierced Tyler like an arrow in his heart. He felt as if the air was escaping his lungs. His words came out, barely a whisper, "I didn't understand it all. The pain was too much, Noah."

Noah's eyes sparkled with a beauty that Tyler had never seen before. He spoke firmly. "Yes. You've focused on the flood for so long that you failed to see the rainbow."

Tyler felt the words hit him like darts. He had heard that before from the graveyard worker. The corner of Noah's lips curved in a smile as if he could read Tyler's thoughts. Noah let out a single laugh; the sound of his laughter different from anything Tyler had ever heard before. It was almost instrumental.

Noah squeezed his shoulder, explaining, "His Word says that some people have entertained angels as strangers unknowingly."

Tyler's eyes widened at the realization. The graveyard worker had been an angel with a message straight from the Lord. *Gabe.*

A chill worked its way through Tyler's arms. God had been reaching out to him over the years. He had just been too proud, hard, and self-absorbed to recognize it.

He held Noah's hand, his voice broken when he asked, "Will the Lord forgive me?"

Noah smiled radiantly again. "Have you asked Him to forgive you?"

Tyler drew in a deep breath. He had not asked.

Noah tilted his head to the side. "Have you read the letter?"

A sigh escaped Tyler's lips. He had not opened it either.

Noah's gaze broke his as he turned and looked over his shoulder- back from where he had come from. His smile was as if someone were calling out to him. Tyler followed his gaze but couldn't see anyone or anything behind his brother.

The dream was starting to weaken. Tyler could feel himself slipping away. When Noah looked back at him, his face seemed brighter. "I have to go Home." He touched Tyler's face tenderly. "And so do you…"

He turned to leave as Tyler interjected, his voice desperate. He wanted to hold onto the moment for a little bit longer.

"Noah, I don't want to say goodbye. Will I ever see you again?"

Noah turned slowly, his face brighter as he backed away. His voice held a depth to it when he spoke.

"That depends on what you decide to do with your life." He smiled, continuing. "Goodbye is only for those who never find their way home."

Tyler's eyes flew open, his breathing labored. He sat upright in bed, his eyes darting around the room. He had been dreaming. It was the most brilliant dream he had ever had. It felt as if it had occurred right there in his bedroom. His body still had a tingling sensation running through it like light electric waves.

He felt moisture on his face, and he reached with his hand to wipe at it. Tears had been streaming down his cheeks. He swallowed the lump in his throat.

He had seen Noah! He was given a glimpse of eternity, and everything about it was indescribable. It was real. It existed. And Noah was there.

Those few moments in the dream were more real than his moments awake in real life. Noah's last words rang in his head.

What did he intend to do with the life he had been given?

Tyler threw the covers off of him and quickly opened his bedside drawer. He pushed the bottle of sleeping pills aside and grabbed the envelope instead. It was time to face whatever was written inside.

With trembling fingers, he ripped the flap open and pulled out a single page. It was handwritten. The cursive inked words made Tyler's heart ache. He would have recognized his grandfather's handwriting anywhere. He let his eyes fall to the contents.

Dear Tyler, my boy,

Tyler felt the knot form in his throat. It was as if he could hear the voice of his grandfather resound through the pages. He continued reading.

If you are reading this letter, it is because we did not have the chance to see each other before the Lord called me home. I know you have struggled through the years with many unanswered questions. Nobody in this life is immune to struggles or consequences for their actions. We live in a fractured world.

A fresh teardrop fell from Tyler's eye to the page in his hand, mixing the ink on some of the words. He wiped at it with his thumb and found his place again.

You have fought God for so long, wondering why He did not send an answer. But He did send an answer to all the bad in this world. He sent that answer thousands of years ago. In Jesus. Jesus is the only answer to your questions. Only in Him can you find peace and fulfillment. Only

He can turn every loss and pain into something of purpose. Only He can guarantee a perfect life once this world fades. Why waste another second trying to figure this world out, when He is preparing a more perfect one for us to join Him in when our time is up?

The words jumped at Tyler. He had been given a glimpse of that perfect life moments ago. Noah was experiencing it because he had believed in Jesus. There was a reason Tyler hadn't experienced peace or joy in twelve years. It was because he did not have Jesus. Instead, he had sought comfort in his pride and worldly pleasures just for small moments of relief. He found his place in the letter again.

In the battle between condemnation and God's grace, His grace will always triumph. I have been praying for you every day since you left home. And the Lord has given me a Bible promise that I want you to discover. It comes from Isaiah 1:18. Read it when you are ready. It's time you stopped running. It's time for you to come home. Come home to where you belong. And if you choose to do so, the home your heart always desired is now yours, just as we always planned. I kept my side of the deal.

Tyler felt his breath catch in his throat. He stared at the last few words. He had to read it a few times. His grandfather's home was now his home? A prickling sensation ran through his body. A weak sensation crippled him. He slowly sunk to the floor, his back against the bed. He stared at the words in shock. His grandfather had not forgotten. Tyler couldn't control the sad gasp that escaped his lips. His grandfather had left him an inheritance- one that Tyler didn't think he deserved. He blinked back the tears and read the last few words in the letter.

And when you go back home, just know that Noah and I will be front row in Heaven at the most magnificent celebration ever. Because His Word says that all of Heaven rejoices at even one sinner who repents. So repent and return, Tyler. There is no condemnation for those who are in Christ Jesus. Man may give up, and man may stop waiting, but the Lord will never stop waiting for you.

Tyler ran his hand through his hair; the sobs engulfing his body. Everything he had carried within him for years overflowed. His father had read the story about the lost sheep to him before he had left. The shepherd had left the ninety-nine to pursue the one. That was what God's love was all about. The *one* mattered.

Was repentance all it took to be whole again? The clean slate he had been wondering about for years, was found in Jesus.

All he had to do was surrender his heart. And repent.

Tyler stared at the letter through his blurry vision. He let his eyes scroll a few lines higher. It fell on the Bible verse his grandfather wanted him to read. Tyler didn't have a Bible, so he grabbed his phone from his bedside table and searched Isaiah 1:18 on the internet.

The scripture immediately loaded. The words caused a surging current to go through his body.

Come now, and let us reason together, saieth the Lord: though your sins be as scarlet, they shall be as white as snow; though they be red as crimson, they shall be as wool. — Isaiah 1:18

Tyler felt winded. The words screamed at him. He had heard all those words before.

Noah was right- God had been calling him to repentance for a long time. The voice he had been hearing was the prompting of the Holy Spirit to find peace and redemption in Jesus. But, he had chosen to focus on the enemy's voice instead.

Tyler scanned the verse again, and that's when something else struck him like lightning. The verse was from the book of Isaiah. Chapter 1. Verse 18.

He looked at the numbers again. His heart started to race.

Why is that so familiar? Tyler thought.

His eyes found the time on the top of his cellphone screen. He stared at the digits. It stared right back at him- just like it had done countless of times from the night of the accident.

01:18.

<h1 style="text-align:center">Twenty Three</h1>

Michael walked around the church building, inspecting some of the construction that was underway.

He dusted his hands on his jeans and gave a thumbs up to one of the workers. "It's looking great, Phil! We can wrap this up tomorrow after the service." The man returned Michael's thumbs up and started making his way down the ladder.

The air was crisp, and the sunlight was streaming through the trees, leaving tunnels of sunshine around the yard. Michael took a deep breath as the breeze enveloped him. It had been three weeks since Tyler had left their home again. In the first week, Tyler had messaged them a few times, checking in. But in the last week, Michael and Beth had not heard from him.

It was as if he had blended back into his old life as a stranger.

Michael wondered if Tyler had even opened his grandfather's letter as yet. He was eagerly awaiting the phone to ring for his son to tell them what was to come of Bill's property. It saddened them to think the house could be sold to someone else, all because Tyler couldn't let go of his past pain and embrace a new future.

Michael wandered to the front of the church and took in the empty seats as he made his way down the aisle. Every time he looked around the inside of the church, he questioned when the day would arrive when Tyler would willingly step foot back in. His eyes looked upon the cross at the front of the church. The words of the scripture moved him again.

And now these three remain: faith, hope and love. But the greatest of these is love- 1 Corinthians 13:13.

His eyes grew moist. It was Beth's favorite verse. She always said that it reminded her of her heart's greatest desires. Faith, that God would get them through anything. Hope, that things would change for the better.

And for Tyler to remember the greatest love of all.

He recalled the feel of Tyler in his arms on the day he had left. It was a moment Michael would never forget. He could feel the weight of the world on his son's shoulders, and he would have done anything to comfort him. Even at thirty-one years old, Tyler had sobbed and held onto him like a child would. Michael's heart had felt as if it was having an outside body experience, breaking in pieces for his youngest boy. He wanted to trade places with him, and rid him of his guilt.

But Michael knew that only God could do that if Tyler surrendered to Him.

Michael strolled around the first row and shoved his hands in his pocket, looking up at the ceiling. *Lord, our hope is still in You,* he thought.

He was about to turn around to head home to Beth when he heard footsteps behind him. He looked over his shoulder, expecting to see the group of workers ready to collect their pay.

Instead, Michael's body froze.

He could hardly utter the words out his mouth at the sight before him.

"Tyler…" He took a breath. "What are you doing here?"

Tyler had been watching his father for a few moments from the back of the church. His cab had pulled in ten minutes ago, and he had taken that time to gather himself outside the building. The name of the church rang true now more than ever— *The Father's House.*

An exhilarating rush worked its way through his body as he looked at the words. Weeks ago, the name of the church had made him angry. Now, it filled him with hope. He slowly made his way into the church, each footstep feeling like a lifetime that had passed.

Now that he was standing face to face with his father, he couldn't contain the emotion swelling within him. He took a step forward, his voice thick as he said, "I saw Noah, Dad." It was all he could muster at first.

He watched his father's expression lift; his eyes were bright and intrigued at his comment. "What do you mean, you saw Noah?"

Tyler smiled. "In a dream. He's with the Lord, Dad." Tyler swallowed the lump in his throat. "He looked so great. He said he wouldn't want to be anywhere else." He let out a single laugh. "He knocked some sense into me. As he always did."

The tears welled up in his father's eyes as he stepped forward. "We always knew that's where Noah was, Son. I'm just glad you know that now, too." He paused, smiling. "And why are you here, Son? What has happened?"

Tyler took a few steps forward and searched his father's tear-filled eyes. He smiled. "Grace happened, Dad."

He saw the words move his father. His father let out a breath, a slight frown etching itself across his brow.

Tyler nodded slowly. "I'm tired of running. I'm tired of fighting. I've asked the Lord to forgive me for everything. And I know He has. I felt it the moment I repented." Before Tyler saw it coming, his father closed the distance between them and threw his arms around him tightly.

The embrace felt like an eternity of emotions that were pent up for years, waiting for this one moment. Tyler clung onto his father and felt the tears pool his vision.

"Thank you, Dad," His voice trailed off as he continued, "For always hoping. For always praying. For always waiting."

He felt his father's hand on the back of his head, ruffling the base of his neck. His father's voice sounded overwhelmed. "You're home now, Son. The season of waiting is over."

Tyler pulled back and saw his father's red eyes. He smiled and wiped at his father's tears before reaching into his jean pocket to pull out the folded letter.

His father's eyes fell to the letter as Tyler held it up, saying, "You and Mom knew all this time."

His father smiled. "It wasn't our news to tell. God's timing is perfect."

Tyler let out a single laugh. "This last week has been the most peaceful week I have had in twelve years. You know why?"

His father's eyes gleamed. "Why, Son?"

Tyler touched his chest where his heart was. "Because I found the Prince of Peace." He smiled through his tears. "I always believed He had more plans in store for Noah, and that I had nothing in me to give."

Tyler watched the compassion fall across his father's face. His father touched his shoulder, saying, "I always taught everyone to look at the glass half-full in life, Tyler. But do you know what is significant about that message?"

Tyler hung on his father's every word. His father took his hands in his, explaining, "The Lord can only fill to the brim that which is empty." His father let out a slight chuckle. "And besides, the Lord always has a special blessing in store for the youngest son."

A warmth radiated Tyler's inner being at his father's words. His grandfather had taught him that. For years, Tyler had felt empty and exhausted. Now that he had surrendered, he knew that the Lord would fill his cup to overflow.

His father grinned, his tone light-hearted. "Now, it's time to find your mother." He paused, grinning. "And Emily."

Tyler felt his breath catch in his throat at the sound of her name. He let his eyes fall to the ground, saying, "Dad, it was Emily who reminded me of something very important." He thought back to the day and felt a stirring within him.

"Living my life without the person I love is nothing compared to living without the One who is Life itself. That's Jesus."

His father let out a single laugh. "That sounds a lot like Emily."

Tyler kept his tone even. "I always thought that Emily was the greatest love I had left behind all those years ago. But, she wasn't. His love is what I had left behind." Tyler cleared his throat. "I was that one lost sheep His Word speaks about. He relentlessly pursued me. And now that I've been found, I'm home. That's all I'm grateful for. I love Emily enough to let her be happy with whatever decision she has made."

A look of amusement etched itself across his father's face. Tyler wasn't sure why. His father reached out and took his hand before he spoke.

"Then, in that case Son, there's something you need to know about a decision she made…"

Twenty Four

Emily wasn't planning on going to the coffee shop on her day off. But when Candice had called earlier that morning informing her of an urgent delivery to attend to, Emily decided to fit it into her schedule. She had a few errands to run and she needed to prepare for the upcoming youth camp. It was something she was excited about getting her hands on.

Before ending the engagement, her days were consumed with wedding planning. Despite the brokenness in her heart, she was looking forward to re-centering her life and focusing on what God really had for her.

The café was crawling as she entered. Some of her usual customers greeted and waved as she made her way to the back. Candice and the trainee had their hands full, but when Candice saw her, her eyes lit up in a unique way.

"Hey, Em! Thank you so much for doing this. The details are on the counter." She nodded towards the side counter. Emily blew at a wisp of her hair as she squeezed past a server who was rushing to another table.

"When did this order come in?" She read through the contents of the order and raised her eyebrows. Something didn't look right with it.

"Ten portions of pancakes?" Emily frowned and shouted for Candice over her shoulder. "Candice, is this order correct? There are orders for cinnamon, blueberry, pumpkin, apple spiced, and banana pancakes. Does that sound right to you?"

Candice walked over and shrugged, looking down at the written order.

"Emily, I don't ask customers about their weird cravings. Maybe someone is throwing a breakfast pancake party."

Emily stared at her friend. "At three-thirty in the afternoon? Are you sure our new girl didn't take this order down incorrectly? It would be embarrassing if it's wrong."

A huff came from Candice. "I took the order, and it's right. Look, Em, can you take it to the address or not?"

Emily checked the address for delivery. "That's strange…" She spoke to herself, but Candice had overheard her.

"Now what Emily? You have a problem with the address too? It's like five minutes away from the church."

Emily shook her head. "No, it's not that," She looked at Candice perplexed. "This is Uncle Bill's home address. Are you sure you took it down correctly? Nobody is staying at the house, from what I know."

Candice looked irritated as she threw her hands up in the air.

"Well, there could be many reasons for that. Either Pastor Mike and Beth are feeling for a pancake afternoon, or maybe a new family has moved in and are jet-lagged and want their breakfast now!" She checked her watch dramatically. "But, I'm sure they will have it for dinner at your speed."

Emily let out a light chuckle and grabbed the boxes from the counter. "Okay, Boss, I'm on it." Before she could hurry out, she noticed something flicker across Candice's face. She made a mental note to later ask her what was up her sleeve.

Once Emily got back in the car, she glanced at the address again to make sure she had read it correctly. She had. She paused for a moment, wondering whether Candice was right. Maybe Uncle Bill's home was being used as a holiday home for a family. It wasn't her business to have asked Beth what was going to happen with the house, but she figured the order explained it.

She pulled out of the driveway and made her way there.

The day was cool, a light breeze making its way through the open space of her window. It had rained earlier that morning for a few minutes before clearing up again. Emily enjoyed the smell of the rain off the pavement. She thanked God for the day. Even amidst many burdens, there was beauty all around her.

She took a shortcut and turned onto the road that led to Uncle Bill's home. She could see the house in the distance, the way its white fence wrapped perfectly around it, and how the porch always stood out, inviting people for lemonades and a good book to read on it. Many of her days had been spent there with Noah and Tyler. Their best memories and adventures were at Uncle

Bill's house. She couldn't recall the last time she had been through its gates.

She slowed down as a few kids crossed the street in the distance. They gave her a light wave as they hurried off onto the sidewalk. Emily watched them go, and her heart fluttered. She wondered if she would ever have the opportunity to be a mother and watch her kids grow up in the neighborhood as she had. For now, she was grateful for the youth kids. They were the ones she was investing in.

Emily approached the driveway and noticed the front gate was already opened. Pastor Mike and Beth's vehicle was parked to the side of the house.

Maybe they are having some kind of meeting or counseling session, Emily thought. She ran her hand through her hair and got off the car. She was about to reach for the back door to get the boxes out when a familiar voice caused her to stop in her tracks.

"Someone said the pancakes from *Emmy's* were a must-have."

Emily remained stiff. Her heart lurched forward as she turned towards the voice, almost in slow motion.

And there he was. As if from her dream.

He was standing on the porch steps, leaning against the pillar in dark jeans and a white T-shirt, a beaming smile on his face. Emily couldn't find her voice. She had to be dreaming. The moment was surreal.

"Tyler… what…?" That was all she was able to manage.

His smile made her pulse quicken as he took a slow walk down the porch steps towards her, giving her enough time to take him in and realize that he was real. He was really there.

He found his way right in front of her. She could smell his cologne and see the sparkle in his chocolate-colored eyes. Something seemed different about him. Before she could say anything, he reached out and took both her hands lightly in his own two. He caressed his thumbs across the back of her fingers. At his touch, Emily knew she wasn't dreaming.

His voice was rich with emotion as his gaze rested gently on her. "You said a lot of things to me that day, which were hard to hear, but very true."

Emily felt her heart rate pick up at his words. His face carried a joy she hadn't seen before. He ran his hand up her arms until it came to either side of her face. The touch of his skin on hers made chills run down her spine. He leaned his forehead against hers like he had done the night of the youth meeting. Their eyelashes were close together as he spoke.

"Emmy, you were right. I belong here. Everything I was running away from had the answers to set me free. And now I am. I'm free." He ran his hands through her hair, and his eyes locked on hers. "And if you let me, I'll chase you for the rest of your days and make up for what a fool I've been."

Emily drew in a sharp breath. She couldn't believe he had just said that. She felt a hint of a smile make its way on her lips. Every word he said blew her away. Something had happened to him since he had left- something miraculous.

Maybe Beth had been right. Maybe, God had finished what He had started.

Emily felt her eyes glisten with tears. "What are you saying exactly?"

The corner of his mouth curved in a smile; one that made her heart race. His eyes dropped to her lips, and she knew what was next. She had wanted it to happen again since the day in the park.

He found her mouth and kissed her. The kiss was new, refreshing. In one moment, it spoke more than words could say. It covered all they had lost, but sparked new hope for the future and what would be.

He pulled back from her lips and drew her closer to him, his arms enveloping her as his face nuzzled her hair.

His voice was hoarse from his emotions as he said, "Even when I thought I was too far gone, the Lord reminded me that I was never forgotten."

Emily felt a stirring inside of her. She looked up at him, her voice overcome with emotion. "So, you're not here to say good-bye again?"

Tyler's eyes softened. "Goodbyes are for those who never find their way home." He smiled. "And I'm home." He pulled back and looked behind him at the house. "This is now my home…"

Emily's eyes grew wide at the realization of his words. His childhood dream was now a reality. She became choked with emotion as the impact of his words settled in her heart.

He touched her face tenderly and tucked the hair behind her ear, whispering near her, "Someone once said to me that there is no better place than a home." He smiled, touching his lips to hers again. "I want that with you, Emmy. Just as we always planned."

Emily couldn't contain the tears. They rolled down her face as she threw her arms around his neck. He lifted her off the ground in a light twirl, his laughter music to her ears. She felt as if she were in a dream. If she was, she didn't want to wake up.

He planted her back on her feet as she looked up at him, amazed. "I can't believe this! Are you sure about all of this?" She didn't know why she had asked him that, but the joy was bursting out of her.

He chuckled and pulled her closer. "I love you, Emmy. Even when I was not sure about much, I was always sure about that." He pulled back, staring intently into her eyes as he asked, "So, what do you say, Emmy?"

His eyes drank her in, as he continued, "Can I spend the rest of my life making it up to you? Loving you? Serving God with you? Finding all the treasures in the darkness, and the riches hidden in the secret places of our lives together?"

Emily felt the tears stream down her face. She was overcome with emotion. She touched the side of his face and gave him an answer that she had once said to him on a little bench outside the church, before their first kiss, when they were just fifteen years old.

This time, her words meant more.

"Yes, you can…"

Beth dabbed at her tears as she stood against her husband, his arm around her on the porch of Tyler's new home.

She sniffed and looked at Michael. "Isn't this beautiful? So many miracles are playing out right in front of our eyes. God is so good."

Michael wiped at a stray tear of his and pulled her closer. Tyler and Emily were wrapped in each other's arms on the driveway like teenagers, basking in the joy of the day that the Lord had made.

Michael's voice was filled with emotion. "God truly pursues the lost relentlessly. Even more than we do."

Beth felt moved at the words. Michael suddenly drew in a sharp breath, and Beth looked up at him, asking, "What is it?"

Michael's face flashed with awe. He pointed out at the afternoon sky in the distance. Beth followed his direction and felt her heart flutter. In the distance was the faintest rainbow piercing the clouds, filled with pink and red hues.

Emily and Tyler were too caught up with one another to have noticed it. Michael took a deep breath, saying, "The flood is over, Beth. This is a new season."

Beth let out a mixture of a laugh and a cry. In twelve years, she had never felt such happiness. She spoke through the tears. "You know, your father was right, Michael..."

Michael looked at her, curious. She had never shared Bill's words with her husband until now. She put her hand on his chest as she looked out at Tyler and Emily.

"In the fight between condemnation and grace, God's grace will always triumph." She smiled at Michael and nodded towards

Tyler.

"And a true son will always find his way home…"

THE END

A Letter From The Author

Dear Reader Friends,

From the time I was a little girl, I had this dream to write novels that would point to Jesus within their stories and characters. I had read hundreds of Christian Fiction novels, and I marveled at how the Lord was able to use the gift of creative writing to bring forth stories that changed peoples lives and drew them closer to God and His plans for them. After all, creativity comes from the only Creator!

After connecting to The SuperNatural Church of Jesus Christ, and after a dynamic prophetic word from the Lord in 2019 through His servant, Prophet Adrian EliJAH Robert, I watched the Lord unravel everything that He had promised to do with speed and favor.

Away From Yesterday is sure to remind people about

God's relentless love and grace. Before I knew it, and within the space of a few weeks, all these characters and their stories came to life on the page in front of me. And they can resonate with so many people because everybody has experienced some form of tragedy, loss, heartbreak and shame in their life. Everyone has felt lost or undeserving at some point.

Just like the character in this story, many are living in a web of condemnation over their past mistakes and sins. Many have walked away from the love of God because the enemy has lied to them, telling them that they are too far gone or have been forgotten.

As I wrote each chapter, I prayed that God would speak to the inner most chambers of your heart for whatever situation you are facing- whether it is from a broken relationship, a weakness, a mistake in your past, a broken dream, or even the loss of a loved one that you still cannot understand.

Like that lost sheep or lost coin in the Bible, the Lord will pursue you and reach out to you in many ways. He does not delight in one person perishing. All of Heaven rejoices when one lost soul comes back to Him- that is how special and loved you are.

It is on you to heed His voice. Rejecting Jesus and His love for you will only result in a lost eternity. And this life is too short for you to gamble with your eternity, or getting caught up with earthly pleasures. If you are seeking a perfect world, with no pain and no questions, you will never find it here. We live in a fractured world; one that is broken because of sin and darkness. But Jesus is the true Light, and the only answer. It is for that reason that He came to die for us, so that believing in Him will restore us to Him in an eternity that is beyond our greatest expectations and understanding.

The enemy seeks to bring destruction, bondage and hopelessness. But Jesus desires to bring you a destiny, beauty from the ashes, and a hope for the future. Even if you were the only person on earth, He would still die for you.

We so often hear the words "move forward" or "do not look back", and as much as that is true, there are times when we are the ones who have moved away from God and need to return to Him- much like the prodigal son. We need to go back- back to the beginning where it all went wrong. As long as you have breath in you, you can always come back to the Father and He will always take you back. Man may forget you. Man may walk away from you. Man may give up on you. But there is One who never will.

A character in this novel asked a very poignant question- *Why do you choose to carry all this hurt on your shoulders, when He carried the cross for you?*

As much as people feel they cannot live without another person in their life, or that they are nothing without that job, or their wealth, or their fame or achievements… there is something that is much worse.

Living your life without Jesus.

Only in Him, can you experience true grace and fulfillment. And to encounter true grace, you have to truly repent and truly walk with Him. And because He lives, we have a hope for tomorrow. You may have found it difficult to build your life on the death of many of your dreams, hopes and seasons that have passed. But, today I want to encourage you that you can build your life on the death and resurrection of Jesus Christ.

Away From Yesterday was my first novel, and will always hold a special place in my heart for what the Lord taught me through it. I pray it will for you too. May these characters and the lessons from their lives remind you that in the fight between condemnation and His grace, His grace will always triumph.

And that you are never forgotten.

Much Love,
CHANELLE

Other Books By

Chanelle Fairlene Pillay

A SHEPHERD KING
*Secrets from the life of David and
the character that captivated the heart of God*

**Facebook: Chanelle Fairlene Pillay
Instagram: @chanelle.fairlene
Twitter: @chanelle_fp**

www.ingramcontent.com/pod-product-compliance
Lightning Source LLC
Chambersburg PA
CBHW031248160726
47993CB00001B/68